TO: MRS.

Please enjoy this story, and forgive the promiscuity.

10-4

The Last Shield

MARK "BAM-BAM" VILLENEUVE

Bloomington, IN  Milton Keynes, UK

AuthorHouse™
1663 Liberty Drive, Suite 200
Bloomington, IN 47403
www.authorhouse.com
Phone: 1-800-839-8640

AuthorHouse™ *UK Ltd.*
500 Avebury Boulevard
Central Milton Keynes, MK9 2BE
www.authorhouse.co.uk
Phone: 08001974150

© 2006 Mark "Bam-Bam" Villeneuve. All rights reserved.

No part of this book may be reproduced, stored in a retrieval system, or transmitted by any means without the written permission of the author.

First published by AuthorHouse   6/29/2006

ISBN: 1-4259-3916-3 (sc)

Library of Congress Control Number: 2006904886

Printed in the United States of America
Bloomington, Indiana

This book is printed on acid-free paper.

Synopsis

THE SHIELD WAS RIGHT!

In reflection, peering out at the endless streets of mile high buildings, filled to their capacity of ageless and corrupted people, I try to recall a time of simple pleasures - A time when youth was sought after with the greatest of vigilance. Old age was feared and almost looked down upon. Most people would do anything to prevent the effects of age. Sickness and disease which once ran rampant throughout the world, is now a faded memory. A tragedy in itself, as it was necessary. I know that now. Whatever pain or uncertainty was placed on an individual when diagnosed with a fatal or crippling disease was certainly a far better justice than we presently face. The lines between life and death, sickness and health are but a distant memory, for those of us who can remember. The last hundred and fifty years or so have past thru the river of time like a thief without remorse or conviction. The reality is; that when time has no bounty on life, the impossible grants possibilities, as the unjust exploit the just. Life certainly was never meant to yield such an extravagant price. Yet the unknown had a basis worthy of that price. With all the discord and strife in the word, it was the hurts and pains that made us who we were. What's left here now is a mere shadow of life…

Acknowledgements:

There were people that have had a profound and distinctive impact on my life. Some still around; as a few have gone off either in geographical avenues or that by way of passing on.

I have dedicated this book to the memory of three individuals who meant a great deal to me.

Rose Young; we lost her to cancer but never forgot her. She lives on in the memories of those of us who knew her best. Beloved by all and sadly missed.......in hopes you're proud of my accomplishment.

Mary McGovern: whose antics were not only hilarious, but impossible to forget! You always had space and time for all the stray kids that seemed to hoard around your house and you made us all feel welcomed. A thoughtfully, generous woman I was proud to call my friend. We miss you incredibly.

My Uncle Patrick: the hard, difficult life you chose for yourself can only be described as Unorthodox. You did things your own way regardless of the consequences. Never will I forget or betray the memories we shared fishing, playing cards, or just plain partying together. To say you were unique is an understatement as surely you were. Never has someone with so little given so much. I love you; My Uncle, my tutor, my friend!

I would like to thank my Mother and Father for the help they gave me in encouraging my pursuits.

A special thanks to Ginette, for all her hard work in helping me complete this project. Her unwavering support and constant understanding makes this a shared accomplishment. I thank you lover for everything.

Thanks to my kids, Eric, Courtney, Michael and Mason, for just being born. You are all the collective reason for my desire to succeed.

A thank you to my fifth grade teacher Miss Velma Pidutti who has helped me with encouragement as well as with her own prowess of literary enhancements.

And finally last and certainly least, to my ex wife! In my opinion; if not for your disbelieving, discouraging, and completely unsupportive attitude, I may not have had the motivation needed to accomplish this 'ridiculous' story. Is your hind sight 20/20?

Author's Note

The 'unknown' has always carried with it an element of consequence. Whether it is beneficial or disastrous, it must be considered relative to one's expectation to unravel the particulars surrounding an enigma. Misunderstanding, misinterpretation and misapprehension have all led to the misconception and more often than not, a delusional conclusion as to its validity. To predicate a solution by means of pure theory has subsisted throughout our history. When faced with an oddity we don't understand or find tribulation in deciphering, we rely and appropriate the so called experts' opinion as fact instead of its true merit; that being specious at best. Only if and when a particular conundrum is considered a necessity to be solved; there by awarding the proper professionally experienced personnel to investigate, can we find clarity, precision and transparency in their findings. This novel is just that very thing. Come join me on an adventure of a lifetime, fraught with danger, suspense, a dash of humor and an alternative recognition to one of the worlds most puzzling and befuddled entities.

The Last Shield

The phrase "Hind sight is twenty-twenty" is used to describe the regret when faced with the harsh reality that a particular choice made was a huge mistake. Most certainly, if given the chance to choose over, one would reverse the decision, vastly changing the outcome.

The words "ignorance is bliss" can be described as the state of placidity, when not exposed to certain information that could irreversibly change life as you know it, and cannot be fully understood unless placed in that very position.

When the day is done, and you find yourself at home sitting in your favorite comfortable chair contemplating those two particular phrases, it is at that precise moment you realize the error in your judgment.... And what's more ... your ultimate judgment!! March 29th 2168 18:35 P.M.

Chapter 1

Growing up in a small town in northern Minnesota, where the only challenge in life was making sure we had enough bait in the morning for a long day of fishing at our favorite spot on Mud Lake, just south of my hometown of Greenbush Minnesota. We'd gone there almost every weekend since we were thirteen. You wouldn't know it by looking at us, that Steve, Jason and I, were such a tight group.

Steve Markinson, the jock of the trio, six foot four – two hundred and sixty pounds of solid muscle, worked on an oil rig with his father Jim, who's only objective in life was to work, drink and talk about his glory days back at Woodbridge High; where he was the quarterback of the state champion Woodridge Mustangs, a task he never let Steve forget!

Jason Tanndy, the ladies' man of the group, could bang any woman in town if he wanted. Five eleven – one hundred and seventy pounds, long blond hair that had a wave to it, no woman could ever achieve with any kind of curling iron. Light blue eyes and a face as smooth as a baby's ass. Growing up, when the rest of us were running for the Clearasil, Jason was making time and nailing every chick in school. But when he went to college, he met and fell in love with Cindy, an Irish girl, who herself could make time stand still. The only thing better looking than her was her mother, Pam, the first runner up in the 1968 Miss Ireland pageant.

As for me, I was the brains of the group. When not studying or looking thru my telescope, I was messing around with experiments. Not an easy task when you have no money and a father that doesn't work. As far back as I can remember, he'd been sitting in that dang chair feeling sorry for himself, thinking that life didn't treat him so well. Like it was mom's fault she died giving birth to me, or my fault for being born. I only knew I had to get out. The father-son relationship we shared was more like the love/hate relationship of an Israeli and a Palestinian. What's more being a little guy, I knew I wasn't going to make it on the oil rigs or as some model. Too small and too ordinary for that! The only thing left was my smarts, of which I had an abundance of; or so I thought. So that's who we were: the jock, the face, and the brain … three buddies who would do anything for each other. Looking back now, I long for those easy carefree days of biking down to Mud Lake, a cold can of coke and a stack of playboys for our amusement, which Steve always ended up pulling out of his packsack. Of course, he commandeered it from his father who had always assumed his wife had found them and put them out with the trash. Oh… to go back and do it all over … yes, to do it all over……

……"Colonel Cobbs, I'm holding you directly responsible to figure out and come up with an explanation for what the hell is going on in the Atlantic!"

"Yes Mr. President. I'm on it!"

2055:

What have I done? Why was I so consumed with the thought that morality is somehow linked with honesty and integrity? My own self convictions could very well be the destruction of us all. Why, oh why didn't I leave well enough alone! Was my own self-preservation worth the price of lunacy?

THE SHIELD WAS RIGHT…….

In reflection, peering out at the endless streets of mile high buildings, filled to their capacity of ageless and corrupted people, I try to recall a time of simple pleasures - A time when youth was sought after with the greatest of vigilance. Old age was feared and almost looked down upon. Most people would do anything to prevent the effects of age. Sickness and disease which once ran rampant throughout the world, is now a faded memory. A tragedy in itself, as it was necessary. I know that now. Whatever pain or confusion was placed on an individual when diagnosed with a fatal or crippling disease was certainly a far better exploit than we presently face. The lines between life and death, sickness and health are but a distant memory for those of us who can remember. The last hundred and fifty years or so have past thru the river of time like a thief without remorse or conviction. The reality is that when time has no bounty on life, the impossible grants possibilities, as the unjust exploit the just. Life certainly was never meant to yield such an extravagant price. Yet the unknown had a cause worthy of that price. With all the discord and strife in the word, it was the hurts and pains that made us who we were. What's left here now is a mere shadow of life…

After our high school graduation, Jason went off to college; Steve went to work with his father on the oil rigs. While I took the only job available to a short inexperienced high school grad living in a small town like Greenbush, Minnesota. I was bagging cow shit for the "Mance Manure Company". My father said I had to start somewhere. I figured there could be worse places to be working than being knee deep in cow shit eight and a half hours a day, all though nothing comes to mind at this particular time. Besides, if things went right, it would only be a matter of months before my program which I had been working on for the last three years was ready to sell. I could see it now, sitting behind a large oak desk, being waited on hand and foot by my nineteen year old assistant, with her puffed blond hair, legs that went all the way up, an ass that wouldn't quit. Yup ... I was going to have it all ... Although not knowing what having it all meant, it was certainly going to be better than this.

While standing in the hall of the auditorium where the world's longest and most boring lecture on human ecology had just concluded. Some of the students were commenting on how the professor mumbled his words. He virtually never finished his sentences. He would just spring right into another topic, making it very difficult to understand the lesson being taught, much less any comprehension on the matter.

"I didn't understand a thing professor Mills was talking about this morning," Cindy said, while twirling her fingers in a circular motion in her long strawberry red hair.

"I think what he meant was that we all have our own choices to make in life and you have to live with the choice you make," Jason replied, standing in that confident stance, his chest out, shoulders back with those blue eyes piercing into hers.

"I hope I didn't bite off more than I can chew taking this course," she gasped, "besides, I don't know what philosophy has to do with being a good dental hygienist!"

"I'm sure there's an answer to that question, but I don't have it," remarked Jason. "Hey, do you want to get something to eat? Maybe we should take a break. All this psycho mumbo jumbo is giving me a headache," he added.

"That's sounds good to me," she said with a resonance of relief.

As they walked down the long narrow steps that led to the street, the echo of the other students talking slowly faded.

"How about Jimmy's," Jason asked.

"You read my mind," Cindy said. "That's just what the doctor ordered."

As they slowly walked along the leaf covered sidewalk, they nattered about the upcoming holiday.

"Do you think we should tell your parents we're living together?" Jason asked.

"Not if you know what's good for you!" Cindy barked. "Do you really assume my dad is ready for that? He's from the old school you know!"

"I see your point Cin! I don't want to piss him off before I even meet him."

"No, that wouldn't be good. Let's just go have a pleasant Thanksgiving weekend. We can impart that info in the spring," she suggested.

With a kind of tentative smirk, Jason nodded, knowing full well she was right. Cindy's father, a rather big man six – two, two hundred and forty pounds, with broad shoulders and narrow hips, known on the "NYPD" as "Mucker" (a name his buddies gave him for the type of cop he was, always mucking it up). Rough, tough, and hard to bluff, confident and totally devoted to his one and only child, Cindy. Yes, Jason heard all the stories of the man Cindy called Daddy.

The pub was empty, as was usual for that time of the day, but come night time, Jimmy's was the place to be. Good music, hot babes, and the sort of atmosphere common to a college hangout. It was small and sort of dingy looking place, where fishing nets hung from the ceiling and cheap swords adorned the walls. A kind of mid evil meets schooner town motif. "We'll have a pitcher of beer and two Caesar salads," Jason ordered.

Cindy looked great. She had on a tight black mini skirt that just barely hid the bottom of her ass. Her form fitting pink t-shirt pressed sharply against her firm round breast. The projection of her nipples thru the fabric left nothing to the imagination. She looked hot and knew it. Jason, meanwhile, trying his best to look cool and not seem too over anxious, flipped his long wavy blond hair back and in a low and sexy tone whispered: "I have a funny feeling this is going to be a very interesting semester." He invitingly placed his hands out in front of him.

"Sure looks that way," she replied while she softly placed her hands in his and sporting a smile of complete and utter delight, as to openly reassure him of his advancements.

Jason leaned over the table, and gently placed his forehead to hers. His hands softly caressing her inner thigh, and in a calm and alluring voice said "I love you Cin."

A slight blush came over Cindy's face as she smiled and said "I love you too Jason."

When their waitress Kathy walked up with their order, she commented "Don't you two ever get enough?"

She was a boorish prude. Not even once in her life had she ever taken the chance on a frivolous love affair. It's understandable. She wouldn't know the first thing about romance or the thrill of anticipation which the two shared. They mutually looked up at her with a lustful memory and simultaneously replied "NO".

After wolfing down their rather bland salads and chugging their pitcher of beer, Cindy suggested they stop off at the apartment before heading back to school for their mid afternoon classes. Jason knowing full well what she had in mind was in complete agreement with the plan. So with a child like giddiness, they scurried out the door to seek the pleasures they were both longing for.

At the pace of an Olympic walker, they hurried across the campus' field where the tall oak trees stood leafless. The sun's warm rays breaking thru the branches seemed to entice them to pick up speed. A quick left on Toll Avenue, across the street and up the stairs to their one bedroom love shack. Their hearts beating like a drum. Jason, thru the door first, cast off his shirt throwing it to the floor as if it was a football and he had just scored the game winning touchdown. Cindy was right behind him, her hair spinning as she rushed to lock the door behind her. Grabbing her by the arm, he gently placed his lips to hers while thrusting his tongue into her open and inviting mouth. With a moan of delight, Cindy reached down to unbutton his jeans, as Jason's hands were groping her breast. Streams of pleasure were printed on Cindy's face sending chills down her now naked back as they fell to the floor. Jason, his hands shaking, lifted her skirt and slid off her tiny pink wet panties. The sweat beating down his face, there was no mistaking the scent of her excitement filling the little room. Cindy busied herself desperately trying to keep up with the pace Jason was setting in getting her undressed. She feverishly tried to discard the bulk of Jason's jeans; however the waves of pleasure he was inducing with his hands nestled between her long quivering legs was too much to bear. It made her lose track of her objective. Jason, pausing for a moment to take off his own pants took the time to look at the gorgeous woman panting at his feet. Her eyes fixed on him like a lioness on her pray, methodically twitching in anticipation. He wouldn't keep her waiting. As he discarded his jeans, throwing them to the floor he said "I really do love you Cindy." And with that he laid on top of her, his hands caressing her enlarged and swollen nipples, as his mouth made its way to her quivering thighs…

Chapter 2

"Just grab the damn chain Steve!" his father yelled in a stern tone. "I don't want to be here all God dam night!"

The rain was pouring down, both men were soaked and wet and frozen to the bone. They waited just a bit too long to leave the rig for the night.

"I told you we should have left with the others, but oh no, you had to thread one more piece of pipe. Well look at us now! Aren't we a sorry sight?" Steve shouted back in an angry voice.

"Look," his dad said, "The quicker we hook this up, the faster we'll get the hell out of here!"

The hard down pour had left the only road in and out of the oil rig in a mess. Where there was once a winding dirt road, now was a mud covered pit. The only hope they had of getting out of there tonight was if the chain Steve was placing under the tires of his red jeep wrangler somehow got some traction.

"Ok Steve, give her shit!" his dad yelled.

Steve put the accelerator to the floor, his tires spinning, the engine winding, mud shooting out in all directions.

"Come on baby!" Steve shouted. "Come on, come on!"

Slowly the jeep crept out of the muddy hole which had sucked them in three hours earlier. As Steve powered his way thru the next two holes, they finally found themselves on solid ground.

"Fuck me!" Steve said with a half way grin, "I thought we'd be stuck there all night."

"I think you were right, Stevey, we should have left with the others." his father said with a conceding look on his face.

"Oh well, what's done is done." Steve replied.

He knew his dad was feeling bad about the mishap, he called him Stevey. The only time he called him Stevey was when he was wrong.

"The beers are on me tonight" blurted his dad.

"No, I was supposed to meet Ann at the Drake at seven o'clock. Man, I'll bet she'll be some pissed off."

His father didn't say a word. He just looked straight ahead at the headlights burning in front of the jeep. It was a forty-five minute drive back home but they did it in thirty. Steve didn't even bother to shower or change. He figured his best bet was to get over to the Drake and try to explain to Ann what had happened. By the time he got there, Ann was nowhere to be found. "Think Steve think" he said to himself. "Flowers, candy, maybe a nice necklace would smooth things over". As he drove over to Ann's house he was rehearsing what he was going to say. Nothing he came up with seemed to be good enough. "Never mind!" he said. "I'll try the truth." When he pulled up to the driveway, Ann was already outside sitting on the porch. She had on a short and frilly white dress, with a blue bow that tied in the back. Her long brown hair done up in a ponytail, she didn't have on too much make-up. She was hot enough o-natural. Steve could feel his pulse start to race; after all he had spent a lot of time trying to set this up. He didn't get one word out. Ann started laughing so hard she was almost in tears.

"Come on in," she said. "Your father called and told me the entire story."

With a sigh of relief, Steve lowered his head. Just then, realizing how he looked, covered in mud from head to toe, the sweat of a hard day still clinging on him like cheap cologne. "Maybe I should go home and change. I'll be back in half an hour," he said with a grin. "Ok" she replied. "I'll order pizza."

And at that, she started laughing again. As he started walking away, he took a couple of steps and turned again to face Ann saying "I'm really sorry we didn't make the Drake tonight Ann."

"That's all right Steve," she said. "I've learned more about you in the last ten minutes than I could have dancing all night. I like what I see."

Smiling from ear to ear, Steve got back into his jeep and drove off thinking to himself "You're a lucky man Stevey boy, a lucky man indeed."

After a quick shower and shave, Steve headed straight back to Ann's house, where she was waiting and like she promised had ordered pizza for them. She was no longer wearing the white dress but a short green silk sexy teddy.

"Don't get the wrong idea here Steve. It's just very comfortable," she said with a smile.

"Of course not," he said.

They both chuckled. A couple of long passionate kisses, a firm rub here and there and he was on her like a bear on honey. He never really was much for foreplay. I guess it was the jock in him. The way he saw it, the game was on so let's get to it. Ann didn't seem to mind either. Whatever he was doing, he was doing it right!

Chapter 3

One hundred and two degrees north, thirteen minutes, eight seconds… Enter. Ok, that should do it. Hopefully all this work will pay off. I can't stand the thought of going back to that shit hole again! I guess I'll find out tomorrow. If that meeting with Pro-Communications goes well, I'll be set for life. Just think about it. No longer trapped in that shitty job, all the money I'll need, no one telling me what to do! I can fish, hunt or sleep all day if I wanted … Please God Please … Let this happen!

"Yes Sir… Mr. Keen will see you now Mr. James." Well, this is it. Four and half years of busting my ass working in front of that god-dam screen … stay calm stay calm …

"Good morning Mr. James. Please have a seat," he said.

"Thank you. And please call me Mike," I replied.

"Well in that case Mike, you can call me Dan. Now I'm not so sure exactly what it is you've come up with here Mike, but it sounds interesting," he said.

"Well," I said in a mode of confidence, "to put it plainly, it's a high-tech security device. And what's more, it would allow access to the chip by means of satellite."

"I see, and in what market do you see this system being formatted towards… home security, office placement?" he asked in a tone of curiosity.

"No, I don't think you quite understand what I mean," I replied. "It's meant to be implemented in the computer of an automobile," I continued. "You see, I was watching a show on T.V. about five years ago. It was some kind of cop show, you know the ones where they chase the guys all over the place, when they just stole a car, or are in a high speed chase. Well, I started thinking, too bad the police don't have some way of shutting down that car, and then boom, it hit me. Why not make a computer chip that's placed in the tail light or the bumper of any car or truck that relays back to the ignition and is controlled by a main power grid. So for instance, if a cop was in a high speed chase with someone who just stole a car, robbed a bank, or was just driving like a maniac, all he would have to do is scan the bumper or tail light, input the code that is set for that chip and zap, it will appear on his screen. He then enters the shutdown code registered for that frequency and bingo, the car shuts off, or say someone had stolen your car, well then all you need to do is call the police with your vehicle registration number, they then punch in the code to the corresponding number and presto, the signal goes to the satellite, then to the car's computer and shuts down. Then the homing beacon is activated and shows the cops precisely where your car is."

As I finished speaking, I suddenly noticed the look on Dan's face. His jaw was wide open, his eyes were locked on me as if he was a starving man and I was a bacon wrapped filet mignon! At first, I wasn't convinced how to read the perplexed look on his face. This was going to be the very end of me or the beginning of something tremendously good. Not knowing if he considered me a moron or a genius, I had to play my last card.

"I realize you have a lot of work to do and that you're a busy man Dan," I said in a clear and confident voice "so I won't take up any more of your time. I'll leave my phone number with your secretary and you can call me if you think this a project that Pro-Communications would be interested in pursuing."

A moment of silence entered the room, the look on Dan's face still frozen in time. Not sure if he heard my suggestion, I started to repeat myself "I can give my phone…"

He broke in swiftly. "Am I to understand that you already have this program in place on a chip?" he asked.

"Well, yes," I said. "I've been working on it for the last four and half years."

He quickly picked up his phone and said: "Lisa, please cancel all my appointments for this afternoon and get Mr. Petterson in here right away."

"I have a prototype of the chip implanted in this remote controlled car here. If you like, I can give you a demo right here in this room."

A knock on the door and a man entered who I assumed must have been Mr. Petterson. He was a short, skinny guy. His hair was all messed up, his glasses were so thick, and you would have thought they were made from pop bottles. Dressed in a white, short sleeve shirt and green polyester pants that didn't quite make it to the floor; a textbook nerd if you ask me.

"Dale," Dan said "This is Mike James. He's brought in something very interesting to show us."

"Good morning Mike," Dale said in an inquisitive tone.

"Good morning," I replied.

"Well what do we have here?" Dale asked.

"It's something I've been working on and is ready to be placed in production but I'm not sure what the next step is," I said.

"Mike, why don't you show us what this chip can **do and** we'll go from there," Dan remarked.

"Ok, I'll put it to work".

With his suggestion, I took the remote controlled car **and** placed it on the floor. I grabbed the scanner in one hand and administered the steering device over to Dan to drive around the office.

"Ok" I said. "Dan, you keep that car moving in a circular motion in the office here and we'll pretend that you just stole it from my house. Now will say that you are driving down… well it doesn't really matter where you would be, as the chip will activate from anywhere on the planet, but let's say you are driving down thirty-second street and I just noticed that my car wasn't where I put it. So I assume it's stolen and I call the police. They ask me for my registration number which I give them. For this particular chip, the number is 84808097051. Which they put in their computer and which I will do right now … 84808097051. Now watch the remote controlled car… In about ten seconds, it will stop."

As we were waiting out the ten seconds, time seemed to stand still for me. All the work I had put into this system had come down to ten seconds. Most of my childhood memories with my good buddies, Steve and Jason, rushed to mind. The look of my father sitting on that chair popped in as well. My mother, although not in this world, I knew was looking down and smiling. My future was hanging in the balance. And lest I forget, the smell of that shit house "Mance Manure Company" just waiting for me to fail…

Shit it worked!!!

"And there you have it," I said in a tentative voice. "Now if you look at this little screen, you'll see that the homing device is showing you precisely where the car is, forty two meters north from the corner of Wax and McCarthy which happens to be this very building."

The two men looked at one another in a perplexed fashion. Their eyes wide open, then grinning from ear to ear as they focused in on me.

"The way I see it, with fifty million cars and trucks being produced world wide, that is one hell of a market," I said with a now totally confident voice.

"You bet your ass it is," Dan replied.

"So where do we go from here?" I asked.

"Well," Dan said while looking over to Dale in a confirming way, "I think now is the time we offer you a position here at Pro-Communications."

I thought I had prepared myself to respond to that very offer I had hoped would come my way from this meeting, I should have smiled and taken the offer, what's wrong with me, answer them you moron…….. but I found myself questioning the motives of their offer.

"I wasn't really looking to find a job here Dan," I said hesitantly. "I was looking for more of a partnership."

Dan's face dropped suddenly and said "What sort of partnership were you thinking of Mike?"

"Well, I know that my system works, and works very well. All the programming is done and all the bugs are worked out. She's ready to be sold as a complete system. Now, I know I don't fully comprehend the way things get bought and sold in the grand scheme of big business, but I would like to either sell this whole system, or at least be CEO of its production and distribution, all the while maintaining total and complete control of my product."

"I see," remarked Dan with a note of belligerence. "I don't have the authority to make that type of decision. It will have to go thru the board of directors and ultimately voted on, but I assure you we can come to some sort of arrangement. Leave it with me for today and we can meet tomorrow and I'll let you know what we come up with."

"That sounds fair to me Dan," I said. "I hope we can do business."

And with that, I gathered up my toys and headed towards the door wondering if I just made the biggest mistake of my life. Reaching for the knob, I glanced back at the two gentlemen now both standing and facing me.

"I need you to understand something here guys. I've worked on this chip for nearly five years, every day and every night. This is the only thing I have, my only future. So you'll understand when I say… I have nothing to lose!" and out the door I went.

Dan turning to Dale said "Call Brenda, Brent, Davis and tell them we need to have an emergency board meeting right now!"

Snapping his fingers, Dale turned and said "I'm on it!"

"I'll start to crunch some numbers here and see just what kind of dollars we're talking about. Get everyone together and meet me back in the conference room in ten minutes."

After a few minutes of quick figuring and looking down at the numbers on his note pad, Dan placed his hands on top of his head and in an astonished voice said "This is unbelievable! We just have to get a piece of this!" With his pad in hand, he shuffled off to the boardroom where Dale, Brenda, Brent and Davis were already assembled. Dan walked in the room and sat down. Without even giving the normal hellos to those gathered around the long rectangular table, he started to recount the events that had just taken place in his office. He explained in every detail what he and Dale had witnessed, with a complete description of all the equipment that was used in the demonstration. When he finished speaking, he placed his hands on the back of his head, sat back in his chair and said "We have a very interesting deal in front of us. I've done some real short number shooting on this project, and to tell you the truth I'm nervous as hell at the prospect of getting involved with those kinds of numbers… But I'm more concerned with the thought of not being there at all. Now, I've jotted down the cost analysis of putting together this system based on the materials showed to us by Mr. James. Of course, the cost will be dramatically reduced when placed in mass production, but for our purposes today they will suffice. I've worked out the material cost as follows:

- The coded chip: three dollars
- The scanning gun used to decode the chip: fourteen dollars
- The main frame computer which will have to be accessible by no less than one hundred security personnel will have a yearly cost of approximately five million dollars.

"Now, we all know nothing like this system has ever been researched or studied but we also know that this is an "I can't" lose situation. Based on the fact that there are over fifteen-million cars and trucks being produced every year around the globe, and seeing that this is a safety as well as security issue, I feel there will be no problem selling it to the auto industry as well as the public. With a purchase cost of somewhere in the ball park of three hundred and ninety nine dollars, and a monitoring fee of say, two hundred dollars a year, that would make a profit of…" he paused for a second and in a coarse tone said "Two and a half billion dollars a year!" Everyone at the table looked around the room at one another, and then Brent standing up with his eyes fixed on Dan said "There's got to be a catch. Nobody is going to just give up this kind of system without having a major role in its development or a big cut of the profits."

Dan broke in saying "We know that Mike James wants to have complete control of this project and wants to maintain ownership of his system which, of course, is only natural. The factor unknown to us is the percentage he is willing to share with the company for mass producing it. Without a percentage of the gross profit, it would be foolish for us to partake in this venture but I'm sure for ten percent of the net profit, we would have no trouble fitting into his plan. Besides, he came to us with this. I'm sure he realizes he'll have to give up some part of control. No one could possibly handle a job of this magnitude alone."

The anxious group looked around at one another once again, all bearing a hopeful smile and nodding to each other.

"Do we need a vote, or can I assume we all want to be part of this?" Brenda asked.

They all started to laugh in a gesture of agreement, knowing full well this was the biggest thing ever to happen to them and their company.

"You all realize this will take priority over all other projects and place everything else on the back burner," Davis commented.

"Yes, but I don't think we could afford to pursue any other project while all of our resources placed into this one. Besides, it will take all the man power we have to take this from production to installation," Dan answered.

"So, I guess that means we stop working on all other active accounts as of now?" Brent asked.

"Yes," said Dan. "We'll concentrate on this from here on in. Every thing else is a dead stick."

The group looked around at each other and all nodded.

"Dale, you get the chip production in place. Brenda, you handle the scanner distribution. Brent, take care of the shipping and receiving department. Davis, take care of financing," Dan ordered.

"Sounds good to me but are we forgetting that we don't have the system yet?" Davis remarked.

"I'll call Mike tonight and run things past him. Giving him complete control of the project is his main point of interest and I can convince him he will have it. We'll give him the resources and financial assistance it will take to produce and distribute his system. I think for a ten percent cut of the profit, he'll want to deal with us. Besides, I thought we should give him some sort of cash bonus when it comes time to signing the contracts. That should seal the deal. Remember, Mike has never seen big money before. I was thinking, say two million dollars. That should just about do it. Does everyone agree?" Dan asked. They all nodded.

Nine thirty that same night, as I sat in my bedroom pondering the future, the phone rang. "Hello".

"Hi Mike its Dan Keen."

"Hey Dan, how's it going?"

"Well Mike, we just concluded our board meeting on your security system and I'll tell you, the entire board was quite impressed."

"That's great. I don't mind telling you it's been a long few hours for me here."

"It's been a long few hours over here as well Mike," Dan replied.

My heart was pounding like a drum, my right leg jumping up and down like a jackhammer. A million thoughts were racing in my mind. I hardly had the courage to speak. I took a deep breath and asked "So what's the verdict?"

Dan cleared his throat and said "I think it would be better if we talk about this in my office tomorrow."

"I'd much rather know where I'm sitting right now if you don't mind Dan," I replied.

"Ok Mike, well there's still a lot of issues to work out but we're prepared to offer you our services and resources to bring this system of yours from production to distribution, as well as marketing and monitoring the system. Our company would receive ten percent of the gross profits for our involvement while you maintain control of your company. We supply all your products to sell and the means of selling it and you supply the product to make. You could say it's a win-win proposition. You get your system developed, produced and sold while we develop, produce and distribute this project. We factored in all our warehouse space, manpower and assembly lines and we're good to go that way. We estimate about two months for full production. Now, if all goes to plan here, we're looking at about three billion dollars profit a year. Compounded by eight when you consider the average time a new car stays on the road is eight years. That's eight years of monitoring fees as well. It's a shit load of money we're dealing with here Mike, and as a gesture of good faith, we're offering you a signing bonus when we sign the deal together."

I took in an even bigger breath and asked "How much of a bonus are we talking about here Dan?"

"Does two million dollars sound about right to you Mike?" Dan answered.

I couldn't believe my ears. It was everything I dreamed of and more! This was it, all that hard work paid off. Just think of it, I was now going to be the master of my own domain, chief of the tribe, captain of the ship, head of the class, Mr. big ….

"So, where do we go from here Dan?" I asked.

"Well, I think you should find yourself the best lawyer you can to set up your business. When you get that done, call me and we'll set up a meeting with both our lawyers. Once we have a deal on paper, you get the two million, we can then start production and go on to make a shit load of money together. By the way, do you have a name in mind for this system?"

"Sure do Dan. It's called MayMoo-Tech Industries," I said proudly.

"Sounds good to me Mike," Dan answered.

"Ok," I said in an excited tone.

"I'll see you tomorrow, say ten o'clock?"

"Ten it is Mike. I'll see you tomorrow, bye."

As I hung up the phone, I fell to the floor beside my bed and kept repeating to myself "Two million dollars, two million dollars, two million dollars …." When the shock of the conversation had passed, I took a note pad out from my side desk. "Ok," I said to myself. "First thing's first. I have to get Mr. Burns to represent me. He's the best dam lawyer in the state. I'll go see him first thing in the morning. I got to make sure this is done right. Next we go over to Pro-Communications and sign the deal and get the two million dollars, bring it to the bank and make the deposit. I know I can count on Jason and Steve to come and work with me. I'll call them both tomorrow, after I have the money in the bank. Man, they're going to have a shit fit when they hear about this! I can't wait to tell them the good news. Maybe I'll call them right now." Looking at my watch in disbelief, I thought otherwise of calling them. "Fuck around!" I said, still talking to myself. "It's three in the morning!" It seemed like only minutes had passed by since talking with Dan. I really must have sat there a long time in shock. "I'd better get some sleep. I'll call the boys in the morning."

Chapter 4

With the scent of their love still lingering in the air, Jason and Cindy laid there on the floor covered in sweat. A smile of ecstasy painted on both their faces. Cindy, rubbing her fingers in the thick black hair on Jason's chest, was just about to nod off when Jason said "I got to get going Cin".

As Jason made his way to his feet, still a little shaky, he looked up at the clock and exclaimed "Damn, I'm late for my English class!"

"You better go Jason" Cindy whispered, now a mere heart beat from going under, "I'll see you tonight."

She drifted off to sleep, still smiling with delight. Jason went into the washroom, knowing he was running late already he jumped in and out of the shower. Dressing as fast as he could, while still trying his best to be quiet as not to wake up Cindy. He got his books together and headed off. Once again walking at a fast pace, although this time with a entirely different motive behind him, he made his way back to school, all the while thinking of Cindy tucked away in their bed. Making his way up the narrow stairs of the west side arts building, he ran into a friend of his and said "How's it hanging Jeff? Thought you'd be at the pub by now?"

Jeff, known for his outrageous jokes and drinking, shrugged his scrawny shoulders and said: "Out of money dude, sell you my soul for fifty bucks though!"

"You're such a piece of rat shit Jeff," Jason came back.

"Ok, Ok, forty bucks," he laughed.

"It's not worth a buck, let alone forty," Jason replied.

"No, had a class this afternoon," Jeff added.

"Yah, I'm running late though, have to go bud. See you later," Jason said.

He knew going to class that afternoon was a total waste of time. Sitting at his desk, he couldn't think of anything but Cindy and the way she looked curled up on their bed. Time seemed to drag on and on, until finally he drifted off to sleep right in the middle of Professor Brills lecture. By the time he had awakened, the classroom was empty. "Oh shit!" he repeated to himself. He slowly made his way out the door of the now abandoned class room, he wanted nothing else but to be at the side of his precious Cindy, so at the quick step he hurried back to his apartment only to find Cindy and her best friend Tina sitting at the table in their small but cozy kitchen. Glancing up at him in a strange and unusual way, Cindy asked "How was your class Jason?"

"Oh, I fell asleep in the middle of it," he replied. "Something must have burnt me out before hand," he said as he glanced toward Cindy and smiled.

But to his amazement she wasn't smiling back at him. He never had seen her in this way before, kind of standoffish with an almost worried look on her face. Tina meanwhile stood up and put her shoes on. She was a petite yet athletic looking girl, long brown hair that she always had in a ponytail. Her eyes were a very light green, like that of translucent jade. Earrings filled the left side of her ear, while just a single cross dangled from the right. A good looking woman to say the least, but tonight she had a look of bewilderment, almost verging on discontent.

"Hi Jason," she said.

Then looking down at Cindy and passing her small hands over Cindy's hair she said "Give me a call tomorrow and we'll take it from there ok?"

"Ok Tina, and thanks a bunch," Cindy replied.

"Good night Jason," Tina said in a quick note. "See you Tina," he said.

And she opened the door and walked out leaving Jason gazing at Cindy in puzzlement. "Is there something wrong here Cin?" he asked.

"I think you should sit down Jason," she replied.

He sat down next to her taking her hand in his, he leaned over and kissed her forehead and said "What's wrong baby?"

"Funny you should say that Jason. I'm not 100% sure but I'm very late, and you know how regular I usually am."

A confused look crossed his face as he whispered "You don't mean … you're … Ahhhh!"

"I think so Jason. I'll know for certain tomorrow but I'm never this late," she said as she lowered her head into her hands.

Still in a state of complete and utter shock, Jason put his arms around her and kissed the back of her neck and said "Everything will be all right Cindy, no matter what the result is. It will be ok. I love you Cin."

With that, she started crying while tucking her head deep into his chest. They sat there at the table holding one another as Cindy continued to weep. As she slowly regained her composure, she glanced up at Jason and asked "Will you come with me to the doctor's tomorrow?"

"Of course I will, wouldn't miss it!"

"Good, I didn't want to go by myself."

"This is a lot to take in at once Cindy but I have to tell you it's pretty exciting, don't you think?"

"Exciting isn't the word I would use here Jason, think about it. I have two more years of study left. You're only in your first term, and you have no job to go to. No, exciting isn't the word I'd use. I don't even want to think of what my dad's going to say!"

"Hey, just take it easy here. Don't go getting all upset Cindy. I can always get a job and come back to finish school. Let's go see the doctor and take it from there. I promise to always be there Cin … I promise."

"I love you Jason," she said with tears welling up in her eyes yet again.

"Love you too Cin," he replied.

The two of them stood up from the table and walked to the bedroom, still holding on to each other's hands. Cindy looked up at Jason with a little smile and said "It is kind of exciting."

Lying in bed that night, Jason could hardly keep still. The thought of Cindy being pregnant and having a baby running around kept his mind racing in a hundred different directions. What was he going to do? Where would he find a job? How would his parents take it? Oh no… What will Cindy's father say or do? He tossed and turned restlessly the better part of the night until finally, he fell asleep, unaware of the events that were about to take place that would dramatically change his life forever.

Chapter 5

October 29th, 2004 9:15 A.M.

This was the day which was the determining factor in all our lives. Although Steve, Jason and I were oblivious to each other's situations, October 29th, 2004 would be a day none of us would forget.

Jason and Cindy were on their way to see Dr. Farrow, to find out if in fact they were going to have a baby. Steve and his father Jim were on their way back to the oil rig. As always, Jim was flapping away about the winning touchdown pass he threw to Dave Henderson to win the state championship. Steve was all the while trying desperately to wake up from a long night with Ann. Meanwhile, I was hastily making my way over to Mr. Burns' office. We had discussed the possibility of him representing me earlier that week. He told me to just walk on in when I was ready for him. Well, that time was at hand. I opened the door to his office and walked in.

"Good morning, is Mr. Burns in?" I asked.

"Good morning, yes he is," his secretary Jessica replied. "Mr. James isn't it?"

"Why, yes," I replied with a note of amazement.

I had only talked with her for a minute or two five days earlier and she had remembered my face and my name. I was quite impressed.

"Mr. Burns had told me to just come down when I needed him, and I really need him," I continued.

Jessica smiled at me as she reached for the phone sitting to her left. However, before she could pick it up, Mr. Burns came out of his office and walked up to me with his hand out and said "Good morning Mike. How are you this fine morning?"

Grinning from ear to ear, I answered "Just peachy Mr. Burns, just peachy!"

"Well, then, why don't we go back to my office and we can discuss how I can help you."

As we walked into his large rectangular office, Mr. Burns was whistling the theme song from "The good, the bad and the ugly". It gave me some reassurance that even an intellect like him was down to earth enough to appreciate a classic of that sort. Then again, he did look like he fit the part. His expansive shoulders and bulky hands were the first things I noticed about him. He had long salt and pepper hair which he parted on the right side. You could clearly see the result of the painful years of fighting a losing battle with acne. His pock marked face made him look quite intimidating, perhaps a determining factor in his success. Even when he said "Good morning," he spoke authoritatively. His walls were covered with plaques from the numerous awards he had received and with newspaper clippings of the more publicized cases he had won. Everything in that office said victory. Carefully placed on the wall directly over his large black leather recliner chair was the certificate in which you couldn't help but notice, printed in big gold letters were the words "YALE".

"Please have a seat Mike," Mr. Burns suggested.

"Thank you," I said.

"Now if I remember correctly, you have a business set up in which you are trying to sell. Have you found a buyer?" he asked.

"Not exactly, the thing is, I brought my invention to Pro-Communications to look at, and after going thru the whole system, they said they wanted to go into business with me. They also said they would give me a signing bonus of two million dollars when it was time to sign the contract. Now that's where you come in. From what they're telling me, they think this system will make about five billion a year, and I have no clue how to manage something like that."

As Mr. Burns cleared his throat he said "Well now, this is interesting."

"It sure is Mr. Burns," I said enthusiastically.

"Did you set-up an appointment with Pro-Communications yet?" he asked.

"Yes I did. It's for ten this morning. I don't think I need to tell you how anxious I am to get this thing going."

"No need at all Mike let me clear my calendar for this morning."

"This must be old hat for you" I said with a grin.

"Not really Mike," he replied. "Every beginning is a new adventure."

Fumbling around in his side desk, he pulled out a file folder with the name "MayMoo Inc" in big red letters. Carefully unfolding his glasses and placing them gently on the bridge of his nose he suddenly took on a new character. The funny whistling happy go lucky guy was no longer in sight. This guy was all business! Pulling his pen from it's holder like a warrior drawing a sword from a sheath. He marked two parallel across the face of the folder. In between those lines he wrote: October 29th 2004 9:37 A.M. "Now," he said in a magnanimous tone.

"I am your lawyer Mike, representing you, your company and parts there of. From here on in, whatever we discuss is privilege."

As he spoke those words to me, it wasn't until that very moment that I realized the magnitude of what was about to take place. As he opened up the folder and handed me the contract, the words "$1500 dollars per hour of service" seemed to jump right off the page. Glancing up towards him, I noticed the stern look of a man with a clear command of authority; needless to say he had my utmost attention. Taking his pen in hand I signed my name to the document. Mike Robert James". At that, Mr. Burns stood up and said "Ok now … Let's go do some business."

He grabbed his briefcase and headed towards the door, once again whistling that familiar tune. Pro-Communications' office was a mere four blocks away. Mr. Burns suggested we leave our cars there seeing that a brisk walk would do us a world of good. I agreed and we carried on out the door of his office and down the street to Pro-Communications' building. At a quick pace and in absolute silence we reached the door to Dan's building. Mr. Burns turned to me and asked "Are you ready?"

Although consumed with anxiety, I nodded my head and in we went.

"Good morning, Terry Burns and Mike James to see Mr. Dan Keen," he said to the receptionist.

"Good morning," she replied. "Mr. Keen and the others are waiting for you in conference room one. Please follow me."

As she led us down the corridor, once again I could feel my heart start pounding. As we walked thru the door, I could see Dan and Dale sitting at an oak table in the center of the room. As we approached the table, Dan stoop up with his hand stretched out in front of him saying "Good morning Mike. You're right on-time."

Offering him my sweat drenched hand, I replied "Hey Dan."

Turning towards Terry I continued "This is Terry Burns, my attorney."

"It's a pleasure to meet you Terry; I'm Dan Keen CEO of Pro-Communications. Would you please have a seat gentlemen?"

As we sat down in the large black leather chairs, once again, the door to the conference room opened.

Dan stood up to greet the tall gentleman now standing in the doorway saying "Jake, perfect timing."

Gently placing his right hand on Jake's shoulder, he turned towards us and said "I'd like to introduce you to Mike James and Terry Burns… Mike, Terry this is our corporate attorney, Jake Perry."

"It's good to meet you Mike," Jake said in a friendly voice.

Peering over towards Terry, he continued "Good to see you as well you old son-of-a-bitch. How've you been?"

Standing up with a grin, Mr. Burns said "Oh, not bad gofer and you?"

"Can't complain," Jake replied. "No one would listen anyway."

We all started to chuckle as we sat back down. Mr. Burns leaned over towards me and whispered "We went to Yale together."

Dan started speaking in a serious tone. "Ok Mike, what we have here is a standard contract open on both ends, which simply means we can start or stop at any time you wish. Hopefully we can wrap this part up this morning, as we are all excited to get started on this project."

Jake opened up his briefcase and handed Dan, Terry and I a copy of the contract.

"Now let's go thru this very slowly," Jake said.

"Slowly indeed," Mr. Burns replied. "We're talking about a shit load of money here!"

The whole group started to laugh. As Jake made his way thru the contract, I found myself totally lost. It was all "Fore too", "of that", and "Parts there of". I never understood a damn thing they were saying.

About thirty-five minutes later, when the reading of all the legal mumbo jumbo was concluded, Mr. Burns turned towards me, leaned back in his chair and placing his hands on the back of his neck blurted "It's a good deal Mike, just like you wanted."

Finally something I could understand I thought to myself.

"So what do you mean by good deal?" I asked.

But before Mr. Burns could utter a sound, Dan immediately broke in.

"Mike," he said, "We have given you everything you had asked for. Pro-Communications will provide all the means necessary to bring this system of yours to production. As well as all the financing to produce and distribute the system, including all the advertising it will take to sell to the American public. Not to mention the government. Now for us to make this happen, we will basically have to abandon all other ventures. So it goes without saying this is something very important to us. We believe so strongly in it that we are willing to put the future of the company on the line. Now that is as much of a commitment as you can get."

"I agree," I replied. "It sure does make me feel better knowing you're in it all the way with me Dan."

"Well, there are just two more things to take care of and then we can start. Number one, you have to sign our agreement."

Reaching for the pen, I glanced over to Mr. Burns and in a confirming wink; he was able to cast aside any doubt that was left lingering in my mind. As I signed my name yet again, Dan stood up and walked toward me.

Sporting a smile of delight and said "And number two..." He handed me an envelope. No marking on it, just a sealed plain white envelope.

"Should I open this now?" I asked, as I started biting my lower lip.

"That's up to you my friend," Dan replied.

Tearing open the side, time seemed to have stopped. I looked around the room and every eye was fixed on me. Nervously, I pulled the piece of paper out of the envelope.

"Holy crap...." Oh did I just say that out loud? I wasn't sure if I was thinking that or saying it. I only knew I was holding a cheque in my hands for two million dollars. Trying to savor the moment as long as I could, I kept looking up at Dan and then to the cheque, then up at Dan and then to the cheque.

Finally Mr. Burns took it from my hands saying "I imagine you'll want me to deposit this in your corporate account?"

"Sorry about that, I just never thought this day would come."

"We understand Mike," Dan said in a sympathetic tone. "It's not every day you get a two million dollar payday. But you'd better get used to it, because that's just the beginning of what looks to be a very profitable partnership for us."

As Mr. Burns took the cheque and placed it in his briefcase, the rest of the group stood up from the table and formed a semi-circle around me. A flurry of handshakes and the group soon disassembled, until only Dan and I were left standing in the conference room. "Well Mike, pitter patter, let's get at her," Dan said.

"Your office is right next to mine, let's go have a look."

"Sounds good Dan," I answered.

As we walked down the hall to my office, it just dawned on me to discuss my two buddies with whom I was going to bring in on this project: Jason and Steve.

"Say Dan," I started, "I want to bring in two other guys on my part of the business. Will that be a problem?"

"Hell no Mike, we're going to need all the help we can on this," he said. "And besides, who you bring in and take out is your own business. Like our contract says, however you want to do it. It doesn't affect Pro-Communications' end at all. As a matter of fact, you'll most likely need twenty or thirty people just to take care of the day to day jobs that will pop up. Listen, don't worry about it. We'll be here to help you thru all the start up sequences. For now, let's get you in your office and we can go from there."

Sitting at my desk for the first time was a rush to say the least. I can remember thinking it really can't get better than this, although I again didn't have any reference to compare to. My first thought was to call my good buddies up and have them come over to share in my excitement. However, Steve was at work with his father, and I only got the answering machine at Jason's, so I left a message for them both to call me later that night. There were at least a dozen people that came and went from my office that afternoon, but I could hardly remember any conversations I had with them. I guess I was just too mesmerized by the whole production. I do however remember the last person to show up that afternoon.

"Hi Mike," Dan said as he knocked on my door. "How was your first day?"

"I'm not really sure Dan," I replied "I didn't do anything today."

"Oh well, that will change by tomorrow. We have a meeting set up for nine A.M. We're going to set up the plan for the production of the receiving chip. By the way," he continued, "Dale says he has received word back from General Motors. He said it looks good already. I think we're in for a busy few weeks bud!"

"Already?" I said. "We just got this started today and we're in touch with the auto makers already?"

"Of course Mike, we've been busy. All day long, we've been talking and setting up appointments for later this week. Like we told you, everyone here knows this is big. The auto industry has been waiting for something like this for a long time now. And we're ready to give it to them. It's time to dance Mike."

Trying not to look more confused than I was, I said "Looks like I came to the right place Dan."

"You sure did Mike, and we're glad to have you too. We'll see you in the morning. Enjoy your evening."

As he walked out of my office, I sat there with a puzzled grimace. "Does he know I didn't do a thing today?" I asked myself. Oh well, there's no point in beating my head against a rock. It's not like I understand what they're doing anyway. I think I'll be much better off just letting them do their thing. Besides, this isn't their first barbeque. As I was walking out of the building I was thinking "I can't wait to get Jason and Steve involved in this. They're going to flip when they find out about this!"

Chapter 6

Meanwhile, in Dr. Farrow's office …..

Jason was holding onto Cindy's left hand, while softly and methodically massaging her right shoulder with his other.

"Shouldn't be long now," Cindy blurted.

"Try to relax Cin," Jason said, trying to comfort her. "He's only been in there for ten minutes."

"I'm trying Jason. It's just hard."

"I know Cin."

Jason was doing his best to keep up the look of being comfortable. He was trying not to show the worry and confusion he was feeling inside. Wondering how in the world he was going to support Cindy and the baby, without having completed his studies. It's not like he wasn't planning on them getting married someday, just not this soon. What's more, he certainly didn't plan on a baby. Cindy glanced up at Jason looking for some more reassurance but all she saw was the look of concern on Jason's face. At that moment, Dr. Farrow walked out of his office and into the small waiting room.

"Cindy, Jason, come on in to my office."

As the pair stood up, they once again looked at each other as if to say "Well this is it, sink or swim."

"I'm not sure if this is good news or bad, but either way, you're about to become parents," Dr. Farrow said.

Jason put his arm around Cindy's waist and said "Well is it?"

With the overflow of emotions dripping from her jade green eyes, Cindy buried her head into Jason's chest and thru the sounds of her weeping she said "Its good Jason isn't it?"

It's good Cin," Jason replied, as he gave her a soft and loving kiss on the top of her head.

"The test result shows you're about five weeks along Cindy."

Jason cleared his throat, smiled and said "You ok mom?" Cindy, now smiling thru her tears replied "yes daddy."

"I'll send a copy of the results to Dr. Harris' office so he can follow up on your progress. I assume you will be making your way back home soon."

"I'm not too sure what we're going to do or go from here," Cindy replied.

"Thanks Doc," Jason said.

"Yes, thank you Dr. Farrow," Cindy continued.

"I hope it all works out for the best for both of you," Dr. Farrow concluded.

As Jason and Cindy made their way out of the doctor's office and back to their apartment, Jason kept giving his reassurance to Cindy that everything would be all right. Entering their apartment, Cindy said "I'm going to take a long hot bath". As Jason pressed the play button on the answering machine he remarked "That should do you a world of good hon."

"Hey gorgeous George! How're things in cha-cha land? You're not going to believe what's been going on back home! Give me a call tonight when you get in bud! Talk to you later. By the way, it's Brainiac, in case you've forgotten the sound of my voice. Chow for now."

"Who left the message Jay?" Cindy asked.

"My old buddy Mike from back home. I wonder what's up."

"You better wait 'til after six if you're calling him back Jay. You know how much it costs this time of day!"

"You know it Cin. I guess we're really going to have to watch our pennies now."

After her two hour bath, Cindy came out of the washroom to a candlelit dinner. Jason was sitting in his red wings hockey jersey. He knew it always turned her on although he never knew why. But there he was, naked as a jay bird under his jersey.

"Isn't this how we got into trouble to begin with Jay?" she asked with a smirk.

"Yah, but that's a good kind of trouble," Jason remarked.

"I hope so Jason," she said.

"Come here babe, I'll show you good trouble."

Cindy walked over to Jason and slid down on his lap. By the look in her eyes, he knew she had complete trust and faith in him, and that's all the love he needed to devote his life to her and the soon to be arriving baby.

That night at six thirty, the phone rang. "Hello," Jason answered.

"Hey buddy, how's it going?"

"Mikey, what's new?" Jason asked.

"Well, a whole hell of a lot there bud. You won't believe your ears when I tell ya!"

"You don't have the exclusive on news here pal, life has taken a turn for the surreal here," Jason added.

"Go ahead bud, I'm all ears," I replied.

"I'm not sure how to put this Mike… so I guess I'll just say it. Cindy's pregnant!"

"Holly mud crap bud!" I exclaimed. "Are you shitting me?"

"No Mike, we went to the doctor's just today. I'll tell you buddy; I'm a little worried man. We're not sure what we'll do as far as money goes. I guess it's the working man blues for me. So how are things over there in the shit house?"

"That's why I called today Jay. I know you remember my little project I've been working on for the last four years."

"Ya, I remember bud. But before you even go there, I don't have a cent to give you dude. I would if I could and you know that. It's just with the news of the baby and all; I don't have a dime to spare. Not only that but I'll most likely be working for old man "Mance" before the month is thru."

"I don't think so pal, you see, I'm not looking for any more money for my project. As a matter of fact, my project is finished. But I want you to know how much I appreciate all the help you and Steve did give me with it. It goes without saying, if not for you two, I wouldn't have a project to sell."

"What, you sold it?" Jason asked.

"Not really," I said. "I kind of went into business with Pro-Communications. But there's one hell of a kicker here."

"And what's that Mike?"

"To seal the deal, they gave me a signing bonus."

"Really! How much?"

"Two million dollars dude."

"Screw you, two million dollars!" he said.

"Really, how much?" he asked again.

"I'm telling you, two million dollars," I repeated.

"Are you messing around Mike! What the hell?"

"I know Jay, it blew me away too. But it's real bud. All of it, and I want you and Steve to come in on it with me. From what they're telling me over there at Pro-Communications, we'll make more money than we could ever spend in a life time."

"You mean; they actually gave you two million dollars?"

"Yes, they did. It's in my account as we speak. I'd like you and Cindy to go to the airport tomorrow. There will be two tickets waiting for you at the booth. What do you say Jason. Just like we dreamed of hey bud?"

"I'm not sure Mike… Are you shitting me man? I mean I've got a family to think of now. Quit the bull shit. Is this real?"

"Jason, listen to me," I said in a calm and serious tone. "I went into business with Pro-Communications just today. When I signed the deal, they gave me a cheque for two million dollars. And I want you and Steve to be my partners. Look, I know it sounds crazy but you'll see tomorrow. I'll tell you what I'll do bud. I'm going to pay you in advance for the first six months. Let's say, two grand a week, that's fifty grand right? I'll put that in your account in the morning, that way, you'll know for sure I'm serious. I still have your account number from the last time you lent me some money. I mean it bud. Just check your account in the morning and then get back here as soon as you can ok?"

"Ok Mike, we'll see," he said in a condescending voice.

I got the feeling he still didn't believe me. Of course, it would only be natural for him to think I was kidding. I mean, how often does your best friend call you and say "Hi bud how's it going … by the way I'm a millionaire"

"Ok Jason, just make sure you check with the bank in the morning. And I'll see you Thursday."

"Ok Mike, I'll check. I hope you're serious about this. I mean this is the answer to all our prayers right?"

"That's right," I replied.

"That's right. I'll see you tomorrow."

Hanging up the phone, I thought I'd call Steve and let him in on the news. But after a second, I thought better. No, I'd better just go over to his place. If I hurry, I'd catch him before he leaves for Ann's place. Steve lived two blocks away. As a matter of fact, I could see his house from my bedroom. Walking over to Steve's like I've done at least a million times before, I was consumed by the childhood memories of the good times we all had on that very street, like in the winter playing "Hang on Harvey" with the cars at the stop sign (a dangerous game of grabbing the bumper of a car or truck that stops at the stop sign, and sliding down the road for as long as you could, seeing who could hang on longest). Of course the mere thought of it now seems so ridiculous, but at the time, it was the thing to do. It was our way of showing our toughness. Kind of like the game "Chase". It's a rather simple game really. We stood at the top of the tracks with a hard packed snowball in our hands (The best result was when you could get a little water dripping from the snowball, it gave the ball extra speed and maximum impact.) We would wait for a car to drive by and whip it. If the car didn't stop from the sound of the impact, it didn't count. What's more you got extra points if the person got out of the car. But the real fun came when we'd hit a car or truck and the driver would get out and chase us. We considered that to be a home run. We all shout out loud "Chase" and we'd run as fast as we could trying not to get caught. It was a hard process to run when you were laughing so hard. There were a couple of good chases that come to mind, and a few good beatings we received but again, it was all part of the game. In the summer, it was "Knock & Dash". We'd knock on a door and run away as fast as we could. Wait five minutes and do it again. Childish yes, but at the time it was hilarious.

Steve had just finished dinner when I arrived. With the normal Hey buddy, what's up dude greeting out of the way, it was time to get serious. After going thru the whole story of the past two days, and informing him of Jason's situation, Steve sat in front of me with a look of disbelief painted on his face. He didn't say a thing, he just sat there. Finally I asked "Steve, did you hear what I said?"

"Yah I did, I just don't get it!"

"What's not to get?" I asked.

"Well, first off, you're telling me you've got two million dollars in the bank and you're going make billions of dollars in the future and you want Jason and I to come and work for you… not to mention the fact that the Jay man's going to be a father. From where I'm sitting bud, you're either stoned out of your tree or you lost it completely!"

I knew it was going to be difficult to explain all the details of the deal to him, as I wasn't sure of the whole thing myself. But after going thru it all again, he started to come around.

"So you're telling me Jason's on his way here and we're going into business together. Hell Mike. That's some serious stuff. We don't know jack-shit about business!"

"We don't have to. That's why we have Terry Burns working for us. Hell, he's the best in the business. He won't let us fall on our ass."

"So what, Jay and I are supposed to show up with you at work. Don't you think your partners are going to want a say in it?"

"You're still not getting it Steve, I own the business. It's my choice who does or doesn't work there, at least as far as my end is concerned. But I need to know if you're with me bud?"

"No shit Mike, of course I'm in!"

He stood and walked over to the fridge. Grabbing a couple of cold beers, he turned back towards me grinning and said "Yah, I'm in Mikey, but don't think I'm gonna kiss your ass!"

"Ok then Steve, It's settled. Starting tomorrow, you'll come to work for me. Well, not for me but with me. As a matter of fact, I think we'll open an office of our own. That way we can better control the goings on around us. As for a salary, I'll give you the same amount as Jason, two thousand a week to start. From what I'm told, that's just the beginning bud. Soon, we'll have all the money we could handle, but let's stay focused on getting things in order for the present."

"So what time are you expecting Jay to come in?"

"He should be here on the three fifteen flight."

"Sure will be great to see him hey."

"Yah I know. Say, you know what would be great, going to Mud Lake for the day. What do you think?"

"Bonus idea Mike, we haven't been there in ages."

"Well, there you go our first executive decision. Fishing: Friday morning".

Sitting there laughing together was something totally new to us. Not the prospect of laughing together, we've done that all our lives. This time it was an adult laugh. It wasn't the kind of laugh you get from scoring the winning goal in double overtime, or even hitting a homerun in the bottom of the ninth with two outs with the bases loaded. This was different. We were laughing like two grown men who had the world by the nuts, the foresight to realize it, and the youth to enjoy it.

I knew by the morning my other buddy Jason would be on his way back home. I'm sure Cindy had put some pressure on him to go to her parents' place first and tell them the wonderful news of their impending baby, but he chose instead to come home. I can't say I was surprised; by the morning he knew all what I said was fact. I guess the fifty grand in his account tipped him off. Never the less, he made his way home.

Now as things turned out, everything went according to plan. Well not my plan, but the plan of Pro-Communications. You see, I thought it would be fun, coming and going where and when I pleased. You know the big shot, the main man. But much to my chagrin, that wasn't to be the case. The idea of Jason, Steve and I playing the big bosses soon turned out to be a jail sentence. Instead of having all the time in the world to do as we wished, we were stuck in an office reading and signing, reading and signing. The first few months had its appeal, but soon wore off. Routine gave way to boredom and boredom to monotony. Soon what once was pleasurable now was annoying. The rigors of big business weren't all I thought it would be. Jason and Steve seemed to enjoy themselves with their new found lifestyle. I moreover, was miserable. The next nine months dragged on. Oh, at first I could sit in my office for three hours or so before becoming so restless I just had to leave. Soon that turned to one hour. Before long I was pissed off before I even left the house. Something had to give, and it did.

I guess I could tell you of the big wedding Jason and Cindy had back in New York: A huge gala affair with all their friends and relatives present. The kind of wedding a girl dreams of. Even the baby showing didn't seem to bother either of them. As it turned out they asked Tina (Cindy's best friend), and I to be godparents. I accepted of course. After all, we were like family. And just like he was hoping, Jason and Cindy had a beautiful baby boy weighing nine pounds three ounces, whom they named Mason. Proud as a peacock, Jason would bring Mason to the office to allow all the ladies to hoe and haw at him. I have to admit, the little tike took his toll on me as well. It didn't take long for Mason to become the main attraction at MayMoo Tech.

At that time we were in the middle of constructing a new building. The old one was no longer big enough to keep up with ever expanding company., You see on Sept. 19th 2005, the United States congress made it mandatory to have the MayMoo security system in place in all motor vehicles. In fact the insurance companies wouldn't sell a policy without one. The system took off from there. At first we had two hundred people working on the lines. Soon that turned into two thousand. By the end of the third year, we were up to fourteen thousand employees. It didn't take too long for novelty of the whole thing to wear off. We ended up working fifteen hours a day, six days a week. This is what I thought having it all was?

As for money, it came rolling in just as Dan said it would. There was more money than we knew what to do with. Even with the sixteen fulltime lawyers on the payroll, it was difficult. The first three hours of every day was set aside for signing new contracts. It was a never ending signing fest. Mike Robert James, Mike Robert James, Mike Robert James, it was driving me crazy. It came to the point that I didn't give a flying fuck what was happening. Oh at first it was great. Mr. James we need this and Mr. James we need that, I felt important. But soon the monotony sunk in. It's like if you had everything you ever wanted just handed to you. There was no more challenge, no quest. I had a hundred women the first year and found out there was no happiness to be found in a momentary fling. Sexual bliss maybe, but even that was clouded. None of those hot babes wanted me for me, just my money. It put life in a whole new perspective. The only good thing to come out of all this was the relationship I had with my godson Mason.

He was great. I never thought a little kid could have such an affect on me. I mean I know he was Jason's son, but there wasn't a day that went by that Mason didn't end up in my office. He'd play around with the toys I'd buy him. It was the only thing I looked forward to each day. At first Cindy didn't like the idea of Jason leaving him with me. After all, Mason was her only child. But soon she learned to accept it. As a matter of fact, I think she started to enjoy her alone time. I don't think there's a woman alive who couldn't relate to the prospect. It's not as though they didn't have the money to find a good nanny. On the contrary, we were so profitable after the first year; I had no reservations about jacking up Jason's and Steve's salary. With the help of Mr. Burns, I was able to throw millions of dollars at my two buddies. They took form in bonuses and profit sharing. As for me, the dossier of money and companies I owned were too much to count. I mean seriously, Terry Burns would come to my office almost every week with a new list of acquisitions. Finally I gave power of purchasing to Steve. That way, I only needed to hear about it once a month at the board meetings, which by the way were as exciting as watching grass grow in the middle of winter.

It was always the same. Profits soared during this quarter. Our projection for the next fiscal year is a three hundred percent increase in gross margin. Which simply stated was another seven or eight billion in profits for me to deal with. It was enough to drive a man insane. Even Jason and Steve seemed to change. The short list of acquisitions I owned were hundreds of McDonald's franchises, Burger King's, Subways, and a dozen other ventures I don't' even care to mention. The only thing we seemed to talk about was money. How much they made. How much they had. How much they were going to make. It's not as if I wasn't happy for them; if that was what they wanted, then all the power to them. But as for me, it was never about the money. Well, not really. It was great to be able to buy anything I wanted. And not having my lazy father messing with my head on a daily basis was a god send. Moreover, I still had that fucking Mance Manure shit hole I was stuck at burned in my memory. The smell of cow shit isn't something easily forgotten. So on one hand I had the appreciation of the money and power but on the other I resented the distances it caused. I guess for the most part, I was simply bored. That's why I looked forward to my time with Mason every day. We'd go to the mall and hit a toy store. I'd let him pick out whatever toys he wanted for the day. After getting something to eat, we'd come back to the office and he'd play with his toys.

Jason and Cindy knew Mason was totally safe with me. I had bought a state of the art car seat for him. Hell, I even bought a hummer so they would feel at ease. You know it would take a blast from a rocket to dent the damm thing. So that's what life was like for me. Money and power really didn't do a thing to boost my spirits. The only thing that gave me joy was Mason. There was a time I pursued the thought of having a baby of my own. You know, find some girl to have my baby and then leave us alone. But somehow I felt as if I was betraying Mason. I even went as far as to see a shrink, thinking there was something wrong with me for wanting to spend so much time with my best friend's son. Subsequently, after nine months of therapy, Dr. Carol suggested it was totally normal for me to place so much attention on him. She suggested I was living vicariously thru him. In fact she explained I was lacking the intimacy I should have received from my own father. The case of my mother dying giving birth to me left a void of guilt I never had a chance to deal with. Dr. Carol said the closeness Jason & I shared growing up was part of the reason for my bond with Mason. She did warn me however, to watch for any signs of jealousy I might feel towards Jason. She said it would be the first sign indicator if I had an obsession with Mason. It wasn't like I thought Mason was mine, but we had a standing joke between Jason, Cindy and me. I guess they saw the need of want in my heart and the overwhelming pride in my voice whenever I spoke of him. When I picked him up I'd say "How's my son doing?" or if I was talking with Jason I'd say something like "How's your wife and my kid?" It was all quite innocent; they knew as did everyone else the bond we shared Mason and me.

Chapter 7

March 29th 2018 …

It was a day like any other. The ice which at one time laid three feet thick across the frozen barren gape was receding from the lake's edge. The robins with their bright Indian red chests were seen for the first time in four months. The smell of the tall wide spread pine trees filled the air. Once again, winter had given way to the spring. I loved Minnesota this time of year. The sound of the river's rushing water pushing its way to the lake. The sight of the little buds peering out of the crab apple stems once frozen but now about to regain life. It's hard to believe I'd never noticed those types of things before. I've trotted up and down those small narrow streets all my life, yet I can hardly remember a single spring of the past.

The normal routine of business had become mundane. There was no secret of my displeasure in my holdings of the now enormous company "MayMoo Tech Industries". There are some people that said I'd gone off the deep end. But the ones close to me knew I'd just plain had enough of the bull shit. I'd even stopped going to work completely. I found myself sitting in my favorite chair in front of the television waiting for my godson Mason to come over. At the age of thirty four, I was feeling like an old man, bored of life other than that which had to do with Mason. I never thought it would come to this. All the dreams of the high life, the glitter and gold; the thought that money and power somehow would revive the loss of my mother; the confusion of never really fitting in, other than with my two good buddies. Where did the young, hopeful, strong willed man go?

(Ten fifteen)

He should be here by now. What's keeping them? They're never late. They know what our time together means to me. I'd better call. Quickly and angrily grabbing the phone, I dialed Jason's number.
"Hello."
"Hey Cindy, how are you doing?"
"Hi Mike. I'm ok. How about you?" she asked.
"I'm fine, I was wondering when you were going to drop off the Mayman" (A name I called him to others).
"I thought you knew. He had a doctor's appointment this morning. You know his regular check up."
"Oh, I didn't know. I thought we were going to pick up that quad he was wanting," I said.
"I'm sorry Mike," she said in a sympathetic tone. "Jason was supposed to tell you yesterday about it. I guess he forgot."
"He must of," I replied.
"They should be home in about an hour. Would you like me to bring Mason to see you then?" she asked.
"I'd appreciate it if you would Cindy. I got him that dirt bike he was looking at yesterday. I can't wait to see the look on his face when he sees it."
"Mike, you're going to spoil him," she said as she laughed.
"Hey, that's what I'm here for," I chuckled.
"Ok" she ended, "I'll bring him over when they get back."
"Thanks Cindy, I'll see you then, bye bye."
"Bye Mike."

I no sooner hung up the phone when it rang again. Thinking Cindy had forgotten to tell me something, I answered "What now Cindy?"

"Mr. James."

"I'm sorry," I said, "I thought this was someone else. Yes this is Mike James."

"Mr. James, my name is Carl Lambert. I hope I'm not disturbing you but I have a proposition I would like to discuss with you."

"I don't talk business at home Mr. Lambert!" I exclaimed. "You can call my office and make an appointment with Steve Markinson, My Marketing coordinator. He can deal with any proposals you have."

"He's not the one we want Mike, it's you!"

"Want for what?" I said in an annoyed way.

"Do you have any idea who you're talking to?"

"I know exactly with whom I'm addressing. I believe it's in your best interest to meet with me Mr. James. That is if you've had enough of the tedious boredom of day to day living."

"Who is this?" I demanded.

"A friend Mike, a friend," he answered.

I can't explain the excitement that rushed through my body. I knew this guy was most likely a nut job, but still I found myself intrigued by his audacity. This guy could very well be a killer, or even a kidnapper, but for some reason I chose to carry on the conversation. "And where am I supposed to meet you Mr. Lambert?" I asked.

"As I'm sure you're aware, there's a "G 8" meeting scheduled for the tenth of April in Ottawa, Ontario Canada."

"Yes, of course, I understand economic relief for the … shall we say underprivileged countries, is the main topic of summit."

"You are correct Mr. James. But what you don't know is its all shadow dressing for our real objective."

"Excuse me!" I remarked.

"That's right Mr. James," he repeated, "our real objective."

I may have been a tad naïve when it came to world politics. The day to day bull shit of those politicians was certainly not worth my time or effort. To even try and decipher the lies from the truth was an art in itself. After all, their only loyalty was to the last group or organization that funded their previous election. One day a certain party was on one side of the line, and the next day they were on the other side. All after the mighty buck, a bunch of legal crooks. It brings to mind the six congressmen Pro-Communications bought to have the MayMoo bill passed. I think it cost somewhere in the neighborhood of five million dollars. I had nothing to do with it of course, but I heard the stories. As for me, I wanted nothing to do with them. There were some people I knew that enjoyed the prestige of being seen in limelight with senators or governors. However, it wasn't my cup of tea.

"And what objectives are those Mr. Lambert?"

"If you wish to know Mr. James, you'll have to show up. If you'd like I can send you authorization to attend the summit."

"That does sound intriguing sir, although I don't understand what kind of vantage point I could possibly offer to such a discussion."

"Like I said Mr. James, this isn't the proper form in which to discus such a proposition," he remarked.

Needless to say I was quite apprehensive about the invitation. However, I was overwhelmed with curiosity. I couldn't help myself. It was as though he knew just what to say, and how to say it. I accepted the invite ……. (Hind sight is twenty- twenty)

Chapter 8

When one looks back on life, there are a number of specific decisions that unequivocally plateau the direction and course one's life has taken. For me, it should've been the "MayMoo" system that ultimately changed the way I saw the world. Perhaps growing up impoverished as I was became the catalyst for my new found skepticism. Perhaps I should have left well enough alone and not take Mr. Lambert's offer. However, that wasn't to be the case. Ever since I was a little boy, I always thought I was destined for something great. I can't explain the feeling, just the inner knowledge of knowing I would make the difference. Call it destiny, foresight, E.S.P, I don't know, only that I was going to be responsible.

The next few days passed without incident. The media however, took the "G 8" summit for all it was worth covering the slightest angle that was advantageous to a story. Every member of the summit was scrutinized. The Brits, the Canadians, and the mighty Americans were always under the gun. As far as I was concerned, we didn't owe a thing to those underdeveloped countries. It's hard to relate to a society that falls on their face ten times a day bowing to the sky. Or to people starving to death yet still won't eat a cow for fear of disrespecting a God. That's something I never understood. That whole "God" thing always left me in doubt; the thought of one culture being superior over another - one God being stronger than the other. At the time, I had seen history for what it was. The will of the strong imposed on those of the weak. For all the advancements of science, it still came down to the basics of life. The strong overcoming the weak. For all our pretense of justice and fairness, life still revolved around our own interest. What will we get for the help we give? It was the same in the beginning as it is today... especially today.

The night before the summit as I packed a suitcase for the journey, I received a fax from Mr. Lambert. He informed me a limo had been arranged at the airport which would expedite my arrival to the meeting. Having no way of confirming or responding to his request, I simply went along with the plan. It might've seemed crazy to trust a total stranger, but for some reason, I did. I couldn't explain it, I just did. Similarly just as was promised, a long white limo awaited my departure from customs.

"Mr. James?" A huge muscled bound man asked.

"Yes, I'm Mike James," I replied.

"Welcome to Canada," he said as he opened the door to the limo.

"Thank you," I said as I cautiously looked inside.

As I took a step towards the limo, a hand peered out from within it and a familiar voice rang out saying "Glad you could make it Mr. James."

Entering at my own peril I soon realized we weren't alone. There were four other people sitting in a circular position around the limo staring me over. It was a very uncomfortable position to be in. Who were those people? What did they want? My god, what did I get myself into? Not a single word was spoken; we just sat there for what seemed to be an eternity. Even though I was at this point shaking with nervous anxiety, I couldn't help but notice the flair of extravagance which surrounded me. Twenty years ago I wouldn't be able to distinguish between a Rolex or a well made knock-off, but now I have no trouble identifying money... and there was a lot of it sitting around me. To my immediate left sat a big man. Even in a sitting position I could tell this sucker was about seven feet tall. He didn't look up much, he simply sat there, arms crossed and legs stretched out which was all the same to me. Beside him sat another gentleman, his long wavy blond hair trying desperately (at no avail) to cover up the sharp deep scar which crossed his face. It looked as if someone had taken a knife and carved a huge letter V from his left eye down to his chin then back up to his other eye. Unsightly as it was, I tried not to stare, however I could feel myself glancing over from time to time to get another look at the oddity. Directly across from me with her skirt barely covering up the tenderest parts of the female anatomy was a gorgeous, stunning woman. Her lusty blue eyes shone as brilliant as the diamonds which resided on her neck, fingers and earlobes. The man to my right looked at me as if he had just found a long lost friend. I could tell by his demeanor that I no longer needed to feel unsafe or uneasy about my surroundings. With a simple smile he let me know I was among friends, summarily I figured he must have been Carl Lambert.

"Carl I assume?" I asked as I held out my hand.

"It's good to finally meet you Mike," he said as we shook hands.

At that moment the partition glass to the cab of the limo opened and a pretty but simple looking woman peered and said "Hi Mike, I'm Jennifer."

"Nice to meet you Jennifer."

"Mike," Carl continued, "The big guy's name is Leo and beside him is Charles."

Before he could offer me the name of the sexy brunette I darted out my hand and asked "And your name?"

"I'm very happy to see you Mike, my name is Charlene."

"No Charlene, the pleasure's all mine" I said in the smoothest tone I could muster.

Looking back towards Carl I noticed the look of pleasure that was printed on his face. At that moment I felt even more at ease with my new found friends.

"So what's on the agenda for us today, Carl?" I asked curiously, as if we were long life friends instead of sheer strangers.

"Well Mike, that's up to you," he said enthusiastically. "I was hoping you'd be up for a little trip." with a quick glance over to Charlene, who was now sporting an inviting and alluring smile, I nodded my head in agreement to Carl's suggestion.

"Where did you have in mind?" I asked.

"To our island of course!" Charles snapped.

I got the feeling that Charles was less than happy with the invitation Carl had extended to me, however I didn't let his conduct mar my decision.

"Sounds good to me," I replied. With that being said, the big guy Leo reached out his hand. "Glad to meet you Mike.".

"Same here," I uttered (Although I wasn't too keen on shaking a hand that totally engulfed my own).

Although it had only been thirty minutes or so, my new friends and I were out of the limo and on our way back thru customs. I found it a bit strange that the officers didn't so much as look twice at us leaving again in such short notice. Within two minutes we were walking up the stairs of 747 which had been waiting for us to board. Funny I thought, doesn't seem to be too many people on this flight. Carl was last to board from our little group, as he entered he told the assistant "Let's get going." Looking toward him in total amazement I asked "Did you book the whole flight?"

"Of course!" he responded in a cocky manner. "We own the aircraft."

It struck me funny; aside from the grotesque scar that engulfed Charles' face, not one blemish, wrinkle, or otherwise sign of age could be seen on any of them. Perhaps it's just my imagination. As the flight progressed so did the curiosities. I indulged Carl and Leo in casual conversation not getting in depth with anything too personal. I was certain the real explanations had been planned for our arrival at the island. (Even though I didn't have a clue as to the location of this place)

After a short but hardy lunch, a menu of escargot, bacon wrapped scallops, king crab and chateau Briand with a strawberry flambé kicker

I was in the mood for a nap. Charlene suggested I retire to one of the bedrooms where I would be more comfortable. She led me to the upper level of the craft where awaiting me was a lush extravagantly decorated room. From the silk sheets to the six foot chandelier which hung from the ceiling, it was apparent to me that my comfort meant a great deal to these people… and to themselves. "I hope it's to your liking Mike," Charlene said.

"I can't say I've ever been so catered to Charlene, it's a bit more than I'm used to."

"I know Mike," she continued, "That's one of the reasons you're here."

Walking closer to her the smell of her sweet, lusty perfume was almost too much to bear. I couldn't help myself; she simply was the most beautiful woman I had ever met. The wonder and curiosity I felt with her comment of how she knew I was overwhelmed, failed to compare with the rush of excitement flowing thru me by her mere presence. She had it all… and knew it!

"What exactly did you mean by that's why I'm here?" I inquired.

"All in good time Mike… All in good time," she replied.

Turning slightly as she walked towards the door she whispered … "Nitty-nite Mikey."

I sat down on the soft plush circular bed, my feet just barely touching the floor. The constant image of Charlene kept twirling around in my mind. Sleep finally forced me to abandon my conscious effort and allowed me to pursue a more intimate motif within the confines of my imagination.

A more relaxing nap I ever had. It was as though they knew exactly what kind of mattress I needed for optimum comfort. I started to wonder in depth at that point of what it was Carl needed me. Surely it wasn't money, although I'd have paid just about anything to meet a woman like Charlene. Before I could muster up another thought the door opened, and standing there in all her glory was Charlene. "We're going to land soon Mike. We should make our way back to our seats!" she ordered. Her tone was that of someone totally put off. Her demeanor was the opposite of the classy demure woman that I had met earlier. I became frightened immediately. Was all this just a ploy to get me in a secluded area where they could demand some sort of ransom. The error in judgment swiftly sent a cold chill down the center of my back. Hesitantly I followed her back down the corridor to the seat she pointed out for me to sit in. If ever there was a time for reflection in life this certainly was it. Leo the "giant" as I came to call him later on, sat with a drink in one hand and a gun in the other. Walking out from behind the oak separation wall was scar face himself, Charles, with what looked like an army issue machine gun. He made me nervous the first time I met him but now he scared the shit out of me. Carl came into the room with two nickel plated Berettas. (One in each hand). He walked straight to me smiled and handed me one of the guns. "It's best you carry this Mike!" he ordered.

With a puzzled yet relieved grimace on my face which must have resembled that of a man on death row whose pardon just arrived as he's being led to be gassed.

"What's going on here Carl, why all the hardware?"

"Just a precaution Mike, this is the most dangerous part of the trip for us. I'll explain when we get in."

Not sure if I really wanted to know what he meant by that, but it was too late now, I was there in the heart of whatever was going to happen. The plane touched down and made its way to a ramp. Peering out the window I notice about fifteen other 747 out on the tarmac. At the far end on the west side of the compound sat what looked to be at least one hundred F15's. The east side of the area was filled with tanks, air to air missile launchers, and a number of high tech helicopters. As we made our way across the tarmac I noticed the large commando type soldiers starting to appear out of nowhere.

With panic flowing thru me in full force I yelled out "What the hell is this Carl?"

"Just wait a minute Mike; you'll have to just trust me. That's all I can say… Just trust me."

Sticking to Carl like glue, he led us thru the large concrete entrance that stood at the far west corner of the complex. When the six of us, Carl, Charlene, Leo, Charles, Jennifer and I entered the shelter, the door quickly shut behind us. All of a sudden I could feel a downward thrust like that of the sensation you feel when an elevator starts to go down. If I wasn't in trouble before, I sure was now I thought. It's hard to determine how long we were descending; I lost track. I turned to Carl and pleaded "Tell me Carl if that's really your name, where the hell we are, and why am I here!"

"The Shield is where you are Mike, as for why you're here…."

(Ignorance is bliss!)

While walking across the hard smooth concrete that led to a huge stainless steel door (my guess was it had to be a hundred feet high) Carl and the others shuffled along beside me, like ducks in a row. Carl stood in front of a camera which was the only object protruding out from a solid steel barrier.

"Get ready Mike," he said. "The world as you know it is about to take a turn for the surreal."

With an earth shaking rumble, the massive door began to open. The light emanating from the other side was brilliant to say the least. It almost hurt my eyes, like that of when I was a kid trying to see how long I could look into the sun. All of a sudden Leo, Jennifer and even scar face himself let out an AHHH.

"Let me!" Charlene said to the others as she took my hand.

"Of course my dear," Carl answered.

"What is this place; I've never seen anything like it before."

Glancing to the side of me I noticed we still hadn't entered the entire structure. The door wasn't just a hundred feet high, it was just as thick. Panic once again coursed thru me as I was certain I had entered the pit of hell. I watched the others continue on their way thru the opening of the corridor. Charlene was still holding on to my hand and I could feel the slightest bit of wetness beginning to excrete from her soft balm. As we walked forward about three steps behind the others, she was obviously nervous; however she didn't let it show other than the now soaked wet hand that was clasped to mine.

The travels I've encountered thru my business ventures have afforded me the luxury of experiencing many of vast climates; however, nothing could prepare me for this particular environment. Neither the heat of the sierra nor the brilliance of Vegas could even come close. The scent of jasmine and lavender overpowered my senses leaving the stench of the world behind the great door. With a child-like giddiness, I watched the others scurry off in all directions. How I wondered could a place like this even exist?

Looking at Charlene for some sort of explanation she softly smiled and whispered "Let me explain." Up until this point I've always wondered why people got sick or why there are diseases that we couldn't cure or why with all our medical advances the human body still decayed over a relatively short period of time.

She began by saying "Mike, how old do you think I am?"

Admittedly not being a connoisseur of detecting women's ages, and not wanting to be insulting I guessed "twenty-eight".

A silent moment passed as she slowly walked towards one of the many fruit trees that grew scattered throughout the compound. Reaching up and grabbing a fresh date, she turned and said "Mike, I'm a hundred eighty-seven years old!"

With a "You're shitting me" look on my face, I couldn't help but chuckle. Undoubtedly Charlene could see the disbelief in my eyes. I mean, how foolish could she think I was! However, as a few moments passed and looking around at my surroundings, I began to wonder if there could be some validity to her statement. The brilliant lighting which seemed to emanate out of nowhere, and the cleanest, the freshest air I have ever ingested. To the right of us was a mile long lake as blue as a stunning sapphire and yet clear as baccarat crystal. The thick soft grass which carpeted the ground was unlike anything I have ever seen; not even at the most posh spa or resort I have attended. There were no buildings per say rather small but quaint dwellings which appeared to be made of bamboo. Peering across the paradise like complex, I could see dozens of people basking in the realm of tranquility.

Looking back at Charlene, I asked "what is this place?"

Taking my hand as if to comfort someone that you are about to give horrific news to she said "Home".

"Whose home?" I questioned.

"Your home, if you wish," she replied.

"I'm not crazy am I? We are underground are we not? I mean where does the light come from? How is there a lake underground? What is the smell in the air? And what is this tingling sensation throughout my body? And what do you mean; you are a hundred eighty-seven years old? How is this possible?"

As if to give me comfort in my confusion she suggested "How about we get something to eat?"

Chapter 9

As Cindy methodically cleared up the disarraying clutter that adorned her marbled custom counter top, the front door sprung open. Jason toting a large rectangular envelope in his right hand instinctively approached her and nestled his palm on the nape of her neck. Certainly aware of the concern which emanated from Jason's face, Cindy asked "So what happened at the doctor's Jay?"

Thrusting the envelope on the counter top and watching it slide across the smooth hard surface, finally stopping as it hit the yellow rose covered tiffany vase that stood at the center of the marble island. "It's all there Cin - his x-rays, blood tests and MRI results."

"So why are his legs sore?" she asked firmly.

As Jason drooped down into the antique oak captain's chair which stood at the end of the breakfast nook, he distraughtly conveyed "Cindy, I don't know how to say this," as his voice cracked. "There are still more tests to be done but it looks like Mason has Muscular Dystrophy."

In a state of shock Cindy collapsed across the hard mosaic tiles that lined their kitchen floor. With her hands clasped across her eyes she kept repeating "No, No, No!"

Jason, although rot with agony, reached for Cindy saying "It will be ok. We'll get through this!"

Mason meanwhile had just checked his coat and was happily strolling across the foyer that led to their enormous family room, oblivious to the life shattering disease that engulfed his young developing body. Mason could hear the low tone of chatter between his mom and dad in the other room. When it came to certain matters, they always spoke softly between each other so he had no real reason to be concerned although he did find it strange that his father had a tear in his eye when they left the doctor's office which his father dismissed as getting dust in his eye.

"I got to call Mike and Steve to let them know what is going on" Jason said.

"Yes, you should," Cindy replied. "I better call my mom and dad as well."

That evening while the three of them sat down to a home cooked meal, Mason looked at his mother and said "You made lasagna. What's the special occasion Mom?"

Quickly turning to hide the tears that rolled down her swollen cheeks she lovingly said "No reason May-May. I'm just happy that we are all here."

Swiftly the expression on Mason's face turned to concern. "Now I know something is wrong Mom. What is going on Dad?" "Did something happen to Uncle Mike?"

Looking towards one another Jason and Cindy were dumbfounded as to how to answer their little boy knowing full well that life was about to take a harsh turn for their pride and joy.

"Well buddy," Jason said, "you know the funny feeling you've been having in your legs, the doctor told us that it was a symptom of Muscular Dystrophy and the test you took confirmed it."

"Muscular Dystrophy? What's that?" Mason asked inquisitively.

Jason, taking his son by the hand replied "It's when your muscles kind of stop working".

"What do you mean stop working?" Mason asked.

"You know like when you've been skiing all day and the next morning when you get up, your muscles are all sore and it's hard to walk. It's kind of like that," he said.

"You mean it will come and go now and again?" Mason asked.

"No honey," Cindy broke in. "It doesn't go away".

"I want to talk to Uncle Mike," Mason demanded.

"Sorry buddy but uncle Mike isn't home right now," Jason replied. "But I'll bring you there has soon as uncle Mike gets back."

"Ok Dad" Mason said. "I'm not hungry anymore. I think I'll go to my room and lay down."

As Jason and Cindy watched their son walk out of the room, flashes of his athletic filled life passed in their memory. Jason whispered "I wish I would have gone to more of his hockey games."

"I know Jason," Cindy agreed. "So do I."

With the chime of the doorbell ringing, Jason wiped the tear that strolled down his chin. "That's got to be Steve," Jason said as he walked towards the door.

"Hey Jay, what's up?" Steve said.

One look on the saddened and fear filled face, Steve knew something was afoot.

"What's wrong Jay man?" Steve asked in a concerned tone.

Suddenly Jason's knees buckled as he fell in the arms of his large friend.

"Dude, what happened, what's going on?" Steve asked again.

Unable to speak, Jason continued sobbing as Steve made his way to the family room with his limp friend in tow. Gently sitting him down on the arm chair, Steve looked at his friend and asked "What happened?"

After a long pause Jason slowly lifted his head and said "We just found out that Mason, that Mason has …… Muscular Dystrophy."

"Oh God!" Steve muttered as he slumped into the black leather couch.

After a long and awkward few moments, Steve finally stood up from the leather couch, walked towards his buddy and asked "So what are the doctors saying?"

Thru his red swollen eyes, Jason looked up at Steve and replied "Not much. There is still more tests to do."

"Does Mike know?" Steve asked.

"No, not yet," Jason replied. "He is still not back from Canada."

"How is Mason taking it?"

"As well as it could be expected, I guess. I don't think he fully comprehends the magnitude of what is going on!"

Cindy suddenly appeared in the entrance of the family room holding a canter of wine. "Would you like a glass of wine Steve?" she asked.

"I think you better make it cognac," he said. As the three of them kicked off the entire vase of Louis XIII, their troubled hearts seemed to numb for a short time as they re-enacted a few of the more pleasant memories of the last few years.

As it could be expected, the next few days seemed to linger in the perpetual state of confusion and strife. Conversation of work and profitability took second stage to the enormous tensions which occupied their minds. While still trying to lead a normal life, every conversation ultimately ended in Mason's condition.

Chapter 10

There were certain and definite oddities in my current surroundings. Charlene and I slowly walked towards a large rectangular structure filled to capacity with jovial faced individuals contently feasting on the wide variety of entrees which lined the perimeter of the make shift dining hall. The open air concept with only its bamboo supports at every twenty feet or so reflected a sense of hominess. As we filtered thru the crowd briefly stopping at each finely displayed table adorned with scrumptious and tantalizing morsels of delectable cuisine, we picked out our desired choices. Making our way to a corner table, although hardly detectable, I could still sense every eye in the crowd fixed on us. A sudden burst of awareness swiftly engulfed my thoughts. No sound? No writings? Not even the murmurs one would expect when dining in a filled room? And although a completely comfortable climate, why was I sweating so profusely? Looking towards Charlene with a helpless and surrendering fervor, I simply asked "How?"

"Yes Mike, we are underground, a half of a mile underground to be exact. We are in what we call around here 'The Shield'. This place is twelve miles long, four miles wide and though you can't really tell, almost a quarter of a mile high."

"Who built it? How did you build it? When did you build it?" I asked.

"Easy," she replied. "One thing at a time here Mike; as for who built this, it's been an ongoing project for the last 350 years. I know what you've learned or understood of history is what you are taught to believe but as you probably know, what is taught or learned is not always the truth. First we must go back to the originator of electricity which I suppose you believe to be Ben Franklin. Since the beginning of time, there have always been forms of electricity, such as static electricity. 6000 years ago while others simply and briefly wondered why a sudden and jolting sensation occurred seemingly, spontaneously and for an unexplained reason when people touched or touched certain objects, there were others such as Row Kan Wee, Jet Sane Krow and Woo Bann Sew who studied this phenomena."

"What do you mean static electricity?" I questioned.

"Well to put it simply," she continued, "static electricity and magnetism has always been around. Have you ever wondered why objects like the great pyramids of Egypt were constructed? To be as primitive as they were at that time and to have such precise mathematical correct concepts without the technology of today."

"Yes, I've wondered about it but never really pondered it."

"Well Mike, the true origination of the basics of technology was conceived over 1500 years ago. Working off of the theories and concepts of Row, Jet and Woo and their pupils, whom had already been capable of creating and harnessing a band of static light by fractionizing silk to wool, thus starting the inevitable and certain path to where we are."

"That doesn't even begin to explain this place," I answered.

"Firstly Mike, let me explain. The exact position of the entrance to the Shield is not that far off from mainstream civilization. In fact, we are a mere eighteen miles off the coast of Scotland. As for the construction of this place, it took over fifteen thousand diggers, excavators and slaves and over eighty years to complete it. There were three generations of them collectively working on this deep and wide pit. I assure you, in the beginning, it wasn't as grand as it is now. However, the secrets and the knowledge in which we possess had to be strictly preserved. And thus, downward was the only concealable option."

"What about the air? What about the sun? What about the heat? What about the food? How do you sustain yourselves?" I inquired.

"Geez Mike, one thing at a time!" she rebutted. "Perhaps it's simply easier to show you."

We quickly ate a couple of choice morsels of the lobster and shrimp and tuna we had chosen. And following her lead, we departed the hall under the observation of all the onlookers. We walked swiftly past what looked to be the central command post, so I thought. It was the only concrete structure that I had seen to this point. No windows just openings were I could see five individuals hastily going about their business. I saw what could only be described as remarkable. They seemed to be touching nothing, flaring their fingers to all directions around themselves and with every movement and with every pointed gesture a different stream of light emanated out of the openings of the structure. As I stopped to get a better look at the light show dancing before my eyes, an array of colors which I had never seen before eclipsed past every opening, stopping me dead in my tracks.

"What's going on in there?" I asked.

"It's kind of where everything is controlled," she replied.

"What do you mean? They are poking their fingers in the air. There are no panels. There are no boards, not even a computer console."

"Mike, you wouldn't even understand the technology which is in operation here. It is all controlled by light sensor and beam streams."

Although wanting to pursue the situation further, I knew well enough to leave well enough alone. Moreover, it had only been a short time that I had been here and yet I knew that I was about to understand how far they had really come. While walking along the soft silky smooth surface of grass beneath our feet, yet again I was in complete awe of my surroundings. The crystal clear lake to the right of us with its large protruding fir trees which cascaded the opposite side of the lake and seemed to disappear over the horizon gave me a sense of Eden. Perhaps not knowing the reasons of how, why and when should have stayed a mystery. I was in paradise and that should have been enough. Grabbing the skirt of my shirt, I wiped off my forearms of the never ending sweat that persistently emanated from my pores.

"Do you want to know why Mike?" she questioned.

"Yeah, I don't get it. I've never sweated so much in my life and I'm actually quite comfortable."

"It's the light Mike," she answered as she looked upwards. As my eyes turned skyward, it was as if I could touch the top of the world and yet I had absolutely no depth perception.

"What do you mean?" I asked.

"Well Mike, that light is the reason I am a hundred eighty seven years old. It will be much easier to show you than to tell you. Besides, we're almost there."

Not knowing where "there" was, to the left of us about five hundred meters was another huge stainless steel wall about twenty feet wide and thirty feet high. As we approached the steel wall, I turned to Charlene and started to ask her about it when all of a sudden the wall began to rise upward. Startled, and taking a step back, I quickly realized that there was no danger, as Charlene hadn't budged. The wall suddenly stopped about ten feet into its ascent and out walked Carl.

"So Mike, did you enjoy your lunch?" he said with a side smirk towards Charlene.

After a brief pause and a quick glance between Charlene and Carl, I kind of chuckled and replied "Yeah."

"I guess you must be quite curious as to the reason behind this place?"

"Actually I am very interested in how this place works but more curious as to why you brought me here."

"All in good time mon ami," he said as he walked past me and patted me on my right shoulder.

"Come on Mike," Charlene said. "I have a lot to show you."

Passing thru the large door we found ourselves in a ten by ten room. As the large door closed behind us, I began to get that eerie feeling once again. The only object in the entire room was a two inch by two inch blue button which was situated a foot from the wall on the opposite side of the room on the floor.

"Where are we now Charlene?" I asked in puzzlement.

Walking across the small room, she hovered her right foot over the blue protruding button as she said "The Truth" then stepped downward. In an accordion like fashion, the wall to my immediate left began to fold into itself and standing in front of me now was a huge Plexiglas type window. We were overlooking a huge ball bearing which appeared to be at least a hundred feet in diameter. The object was sunken fifty feet downward with two steel rods jetting out each side. Three red steel catwalks surrounded the perimeter of the giant ball in three different levels, approximately fifteen feet between them. There were two men turning dials that adorned the right side wall. There was a woman clear across the far side of the catwalk writing on a blue clipboard. With a subtle glance towards Charlene and I acknowledging our presence, they quickly resumed their activities. Attached to the two steel prongs were long cables that reached to our eye level, leading in opposite directions to each of the walls then rising upwards to the ceiling and across to a clear cylindrical tube? The awesome light that filled the tube had a bluish green hue with streams of yellow that flashed periodically. The tube was approximately ten feet high and three feet across. At the top of the tube were four ten inch conduits which aimed upward and into the roof of the building.

"And this is what?" I asked curiously.

"This is the source of our energy, a magnetic resonator. You see Mike, as I said before, magnetism has been around forever. It's a bountiful, abundant and never ending source of power in which virtually no maintenance is necessary. The titanium plates that are arranged in a specific pattern within the sphere are staggered and orchestrated in such a way that a reverse polarity is achieved to acquire perpetual motion. We simply magnetize the plates which puts in motion the resonator which creates electricity."

"You mean to tell me that you have a source of power that has no emissions, no pollution and is virtually cost free?"

"That's right Mike. We've had it for hundreds of years."

"I don't understand. Why the hell aren't you helping the world in this energy crisis? Hell, you can solve the world's energy, pollution and economic pressures!"

"I don't think you understand Mike. Do you really think the world is ready for natural energy? Besides, look what happened with other things we've let out."

"What other things? Like what?"

"Microwave technology for one, atomic energy for another, hell that was supposed to be used just for energy and it was perverted into a nauseously nuclear nightmare. We won't even mention the chemical compositions that were meant to re-fertilize the ground and to neutralize the pollutants that the greedy have produced. Year after year, we sit here and wonder how much suffering, how much pain should we allow to go on?"

Looking towards her, the immediate thought passed thru my mind "Who do you think you are? God"

With an almost "I said too much" look on her face, her demeanor switched once again as she took me by the hand and taking a step back stepped on the blue button on the floor.

As the wall closed in its accordion fashion, the back wall once again, opened leading us out into the fresh clean jasmine scented paradise. As we strolled even deeper into the Shield, I couldn't help but feel like I was on an alien planet. I mean everything I was taught, everything I've learned up until this point was incorrect. We walked without talking for about a mile passing by herds of cows, pigs, chickens, horses virtually every kind of animal you would find on a typical farm, oddly enough without the scent of that same surrounding.

Finally I spoke out and asked "So the resonator creates the energy which obviously controls the climate and creates the light and I would imagine powers the water purification systems. That I can understand. But do you want to pass by me how you are a hundred and eighty seven years old. Are does dog years?" I chuckled.

Letting out a short giggle "No," she said. "Mike," she continued, "you've only been here for about four hours but let me ask you: Do you feel more energetic? What I mean is do you actually feel stronger?"

"Funny you should mention that," I said. "I do. I was wondering if it was just the clean air."

"That's part of it," she replied. "The bio filters take out every toxin in the air but that's not the full reason. The light, you see, is emanating at a very high frequency, actually, a very dense frequency. You've no doubt noticed how your body as been eliminating moisture all day."

"Yeah, I'm sweating like a pig," I grunted.

"Well, in fact Mike," she continued, "the light is excreting all the toxins in your blood and muscle tissue. This virtually stops all aging in its tracks. Along with aging, it eliminates all diseases, cancers and impurities in the body."

"So what are you saying? You never get sick?"

"No Mike, we don't. Of course, broken bones, cuts and blunt trauma are still a fact of life but all bodily toxins are eliminated thru the air and filtered out. You'll notice the breeze is constant and always east to west. You'll get used to it. The scent in the air is the auspicious result of the actual conversion of the toxicant carbon monoxide to filtrated oxygen. It's a pleasant residue of the whole process." "It was totally accidental. In refining the process of unlimited energy, the magnetic field of that specific frequency caused the rejuvenation and the quick healing of a nasty cut. It was then that they discovered that the magnetic field attracted the impurities that live within the iron source properties in your blood. By emanating a specific harmonic, they are capable of excreting toxins from the body resulting in naturally perfect cells."

"So what you're telling me is that people here have never died?"

"No, not exactly Mike; Yes it's true, our society has lived for a long, long time; about 600 years. We may have had a jump start of what you would call your modern technology as far as medicines, transportation and energy but up until 200 years ago, we still got sick and died. It was almost by accident that Carl discovered the re-generating powers of light density."

"So are you saying that everyone here is related?"

"No, we are not. I was invited here a hundred fifty-four years ago and at that time, there were but two hundred and ten of us."

"Well, how many people live here?"

"Up until this morning," she answered, "three hundred and twenty-five. We are hoping you'll make it three hundred and twenty-six."

At this point we had managed to make it back to where this whole episode began. The concrete structure with its wide openings was now being manned by three totally different individuals. Flaring their fingers upward and downward causing the same array of lights with every stroke. From out of the small bamboo shelter which stood nestled between two mature crab apple trees out strolled Carl Lambert. By the look on his face I could tell there was something heavily pressing on his mind. He walked towards Charlene and I, reached out his hand and asked "So what do you think Mr. James. What do you think?"

"You know Carl," I said, "I've seen some pretty fantastic and phenomenal things in my life but nothing can quite compare to this."

Smiling, he nodded with a gesture of agreement then I asked "But why? Why me? Why am I here?"

"Mike that is something that Charlene will have to answer for you."

Out of nowhere ten men armed to the hilt stretched across the opening of the one hundred foot stainless steel door. Looking towards Charlene and Carl I gave a "What's going on?" shrug.

"I hope to see you again Mike," Carl spoke.

With that, he turned around and re-entered the bamboo hut.

"Time to go Mike," Charlene said.

"Wait a minute," I replied. "Why was I brought here? Carl said you would give me the answer."

"And I will," she replied, "but for now, we have to go."

Softly grabbing my hand, she led me in front of the huge mechanical door as the ten armed men quickly surrounded us. As I glanced behind me, I wondered for a moment "was this even real?" With a rumble and a shake, the large shiny steel door again began to rise. I could feel Charlene's hand begin to stiffen as she tightened her grip around mine. As we walked thru the steel corridor towards the small opening, Charlene looked over to the gunmen and said "That's enough."

They immediately stopped as we continued thru the small door. Once again I felt the rush and the sensation of upward thrust and within a few minutes, we had stopped again. As the door opened and we walked out into the opened tarmac, the stench that filled my nostrils was almost unbearable. Grabbing for my nose and looking towards Charlene, she simply said "I know."

Directly in front of us was the huge 747 that I had just stepped out of a mere six hours ago. The same adornment of military presence was hard to miss. As we scurried across the concrete and up the stairs, I had a very uneasy feeling, like a target was painted on my back. When we reached the top of the stairs, one thing flashed to mind: "I'm not winded" I thought. We practically ran up those stairs and it was as if I hadn't walked but one or two steps. Nestling into our large comfortable black leather loungers, Charlene glanced towards me and asked "Are you ok?"

"Sure," I said. "But I still don't know why I was brought here."

With the plane commencing its departure and feeling the rush of speed and the sinking sensation, I thought to myself "I hope that I can come back."

About thirty minutes had passed when Charlene finally began to speak. She curled up beside me like a kitten snubbing up into its mother's belly. As shocked as I was at her obvious advancement, I was needlessly to say quite enamored with her.

"I've known you now Mike for three years. From your success at MayMoo Tech to the reclusive man you've become. I've watched all the interviews with you. I've read all the clippings about you. I've even gone so far as to monitor your home on our satellite circuits."

I heard the words she was speaking but could not believe what she was saying. Here was this gorgeous, obviously intellectual and stunning woman saying she was in love with Mr. Average. Something didn't make sense. Was it love or something else?

"I don't understand," I said. "Why?"

"I've been around a long time Mike and I've come to certain and definite conclusions. There are couples at the Shield that were simply destined to be together. I watched them as they eat. I watched them as they rest and observed the little idiosyncrasies that seem to just parallel each other. When you burst on the scene with your invention, I could see the glee and the terror that filled your eyes. I've re-watched the interview a hundred times and your expression and emotion was melted in my mind. Subsequently over the last few years, all that I have observed has led me to believe that you and I are the same. However, it wasn't until meeting you and spending time with you that I truly realized how perfect we could be together."

An exhilarating sensation of purity, truthfulness and hope rushed thru every part of my being. Could this really be happening? Before I could muster another thought, Charlene placed her right hand on my chest and leaned towards me and placed her soft sensuous red lips to mine. After a long passionate kiss, she looked up at me and said "I could make you happy; I want to make you happy."

As quickly as her advances began, it ended. She stood up and walked towards the partition that led to one of the bedrooms. Just before entering the bedroom, she turned and said "You could make me happy Mike; I want you to make me happy."

Sitting there, I could hardly believe what had just taken place. Did she want me to follow her or was this just an intro to devastation and turmoil. Perhaps it was the million thoughts running thru my mind or the outlandish revelations that were revealed to me or perhaps I was just tired but I soon found myself drifting off to sleep. I awoke suddenly to the fluttering feeling of our descent. Charlene was to my immediate right with her arm wrapped around mine. "Wakey, wakey," she said with her bright alluring smile. "We are about to land."

"Where are we?" I asked.

"Minneapolis Minnesota," she replied. "I've arranged a limo to take you back home."

"This can't end like this!" I thought to myself. "Where do we go from here?" As the jumbo jet made its stop, I peered at Charlene and asked "So where do we go from here?"

"Well Mike," she said, "it's up to you," as she handed me a cellular phone. "Anytime you want to speak to me, just press 'Send'. I guess you have a lot to think about," she continued. "I know it's a lot to absorb but I truly hope we can find a way to make this work."

She politely kissed my cheek and turned towards the rear of the plane. While walking towards the door, taking a final look towards her, I noticed a single tear rolling down her soft velvety cheek. As I pulled away in the limo, I recounted every step from my initial contact in Ottawa to my final departure in Minneapolis. Before I knew it, we were approaching the gate to my home. I found it odd that for the last three years this was the only serene and comfortable surrounding in which to escape the realities and the pressures of life. However, now, it hardly seemed like home.

Chapter 11

"Why don't you give Mike a call Jason?" Cindy suggested.

"Yeah, maybe I will," Jason replied but before he could take a step towards the phone, it rang.

"Hey Mike, how's it going? I was just about to call you."

"We really need to talk Jason," I said.

"Yeah Mike, we really do." By the somber tone of his voice, I quickly surmised the fantastic adventure I had just experienced was not going to be the only important topic of our discussion.

"Why won't you and Mason pick up Steve on your way over," I suggested. "It's been a while since the four of us got together."

"Ok Mike," Jason replied. "We'll see you in a half an hour."

Hanging up the phone, he swiftly dialed Steve's number.

Ring, ring, ring, ring, ring, ring, ring. "That's odd," Jason thought. "I guess I'll just stop in."

With Mason in tow, Jason approached the entrance to the doorway of Steve's magnificently marbled outer foyer. Walking along the beautifully designed teal blue terrazzo flooring, it was hard to miss the scent of hickory emanating from the large squared off edges.

Entering the security code, which only Steve, Jason and Mike had access to; it unleashed the grand forged steel partition that led to the inner foyer to Steve's immaculately designed dwelling. Making their way thru the inner foyer, Jason yelped "Hey Steve…! Hey Steve!" Looking back at Mason and shrugging his shoulders, he disappeared around the chesterfield instructing Mason to check around back.

Enthusiastically strolling towards the backyard, Mason shouted "Uncle Steve, are you out here?" A quick look thru the pool house and a swift jolt thru the garage, Steve was nowhere to be found. "Well then," Mason muttered to himself. "There's only one place he can be." Re-entering Steve's posh abode, Mason made his way thru the kitchen and down the stairs that lead to his L-shaped elaborately furnished gym. While striking the heavy bag that hung from the ceiling to his immediate right and quickly spinning to kick the speed bag on his left, he recognized the silhouette in the mirror on the other side of the room. "I knew you'd be here Uncle Steve," Mason chuckled. Walking towards the front mirrored wall which was adorned with the most modern and sophisticated equipment, Mason was suddenly struck with a paralyzing frightful sight of his Uncle Steve laying on a bench press with a bar bell draped over his neck. Thru stunned and unbelieving eyes, Mason could read the horror and helplessness that lay in his uncle's broken lifeless body. Standing in front of his ominous and terrifying discovery, Mason could only muster up the strength to shout out "Dad!"

Sensing the urgency in his son's squelch, Jason came running down the stairs yelling "What's wrong?" but before Mason could speak, Jason could already see the reason behind the bellow.

"Holy shit!" Jason exploded. "Steve! Steve!"

Reaching for the heavy bar bell that lay clothed across his helpless and dilapidated friend's shattered neck, Jason tried in vain to remove the obstruction as he kept shouting "911 Mason! 911!"

Within a few minutes, Steve's house was bombarded with black and whites. The flashes from the investigation cameras that kept going off were reminiscent of a pre-dawn electrical storm. As the police and detectives looked, searched and prodded thru every square inch of the house, they documented every last item within the confines. Jason and Mason could only sit helplessly watching the barrage of activity which was unfolding before them. Needless to say no stone would be left unturned in deriving the solution as to how something like this could have happened. Steve was not only well known around town but was a prominent member of society.

After receiving the horrifying troublesome news of Steve's terrible accident, I quickly rushed over there. "Can't be! Can't be!" I kept repeating to myself. I could hardly fathom the possibility of the loss of my buddy Steve. With nervous energy, I hastily descended the stairs that lead to my lost buddy's crypt. Among the onlookers and photographers and the countless number of policemen huddled together, I could see Jason huddled off on the right with his head buried in his crossed arms weeping in agony. I quickly shouted out "Jay!" Looking up towards me with red swollen eyes, he arose and staggered his way towards me, arms flared out desperate for comfort.

"He's gone Mike, he's gone, he's just gone," Jason whispered as we stood there clenched together.

As a few hours passed, Jason recounted the series of events that led up to this discovery. I remember thinking should I mention the events I had experienced at the Shield but I decided not to. Seeing as there was nothing Jason or I could accomplish there, we decided to go back to my place and try to put things into perspective. It was easy to see that Mason was completely devastated by what he saw. We both knew and dreaded the overwhelming pictures that would be embedded in his memory. With my right arm draped over Mason's right shoulder and Jason's left arm covering his left shoulder, we walked him outside and proceeded to my home.

However hurt and bewildered I felt of the loss of Steve, it failed in comparison to the shocking news which laid in store for me. It was difficult to say the least to deal with the loss of one of my best buddies but when Jason relayed the medical situation with Mason, I quite nearly lost it. Admittedly I didn't know much about Muscular Dystrophy however I certainly realized its dilapidating conclusion.

"Is there anything we can do, anyplace we can take him? Any chance the doctor is wrong?" I asked in desperation.

"I wish there was buddy," Jason replied. "But we've taken him to three doctors so far and the diagnosis is all the same."

I figured this was as good a time as any to inform Jason about the Shield. Pouring out every single infinitesimal detail that I could remember about the place, I tried to convey to him that all I had seen was real. However far fetched it sounded, it was actually real. The discussion seemed to help somewhat as I described the clear lake, the scent of jasmine and the feeling of plainly being stronger, healthier and basically indestructible while I was there. I guess it was a slight interruption we needed from the confusion and pain we were all feeling from the loss of Steve.

"If that's all true Mike, maybe we should send Mason there," Jason said jokingly. Standing up abruptly and striking my forehead with my left palm I exclaimed "That's it! That's exactly what we should do! I mean, really think about it Jason," I continued, "There's nothing we can do for him here. Hell, there's nothing anybody can do for him here. At least, at the Shield, he'd have a fighting chance. I mean, what could it hurt?"

"Are you serious?" Jason replied in a completely concerned tone.

"Yes I am," I rebutted. "You know me Jason. It was just like when I called you all those years ago about completing my invention. I know this could work."

After a while and standing up circling my rectangular oak dining table, he hesitantly said "Ok, let's go."

"Great," I replied. "I'll call Charlene and set it up."

Stopping dead in his tracks, Jason looked over his shoulder and asked "What about Stevey?"

"Look Jason," I answered, "it's killing me just as much as it is killing you. I don't have any answers and either do you. Sometimes things happen that there are no answers for but I don't think that he would want us to be going crazy. I think he would want us to do whatever we could to help Mason."

(...... something didn't add up. 350 pounds, Steve could press that with his eyes closed. It just didn't add up! .....)

We had decided not to drown ourselves in pity rather we chose to swallow our hurts and focus in on helping Mason. Even though the outcome of this decision could not be foreseen, we knew it was the right choice. Jason and Mason returned home while I sat in my favorite armchair contemplating and rehearsing what I was about to ask of Charlene....

Chapter 12

Following the ritual of descending into the Shield and approaching the dwelling in which Carl lived; Charlene gently kissed Carl on his right cheek while placing both of her hands seductively on his shoulders.

"So how did it go my dear?" Carl asked inquisitively.

"So far so good," Charlene replied. "However, we are taking quite a risk you know."

"I do believe the cause far out ways the means of how this must be done. You, yourself know what's riding on this."

Bowing her head downward, Charlene simply replied "I know."

Chapter 13

The next few days were wrought with phone calls, interviews and a barrage of questions from the police. It was hard enough dealing with everything on our plate, let alone the uncertainty of what had actually happened. It's hard to believe that just a few weeks prior to these incidences, I was desperately longing for a quickening. In hindsight, I'd rather it be dull.

On the morning of the third day, detective William Bovin approached me and stated that the position of the police was that Steve's death was an accident. He figured Steve was working out and from a torn triceps, he could not handle the heavy weight which was pressed above him and it came crashing down across his shoulder shattering his neck. Facing the harsh reality that Steve was gone, I simply had to accept it and place my energies onto the task of Mason.

Reaching into the silk lining of my double-breasted Pierre Chodan custom-made suit, I grabbed my hot line phone, opened it and pressed "SEND".

"Ring, ring."

"Hello Mike." The soft subtle seductive sound of Charlene's voice was immediately soothing. I could imagine the very position of the phone nuzzled up against her soft rosy cheek.

"Charlene," I said, "There's been a terrible accident here."

But before I could continue, she broke in saying "I heard Mike. It's been on the news. Are you ok?"

Aside from the condolences I received from Jason and Cindy, this was the only true heart-felt compassion I had received concerning Steve.

"I'll make it," I responded. "It's tough. He was one of my best friends and quite frankly I only had two."

"Well I'm very sorry of your loss Mike. Is there anything I can do, anything at all?"

"Actually Charlene, there is really nothing you can do about Steve. However, I just found out that my godson, Mason, was diagnosed with Muscular Dystrophy."

"My goodness," she said. "That must be difficult."

"Yes, it is," I replied. "What started out to be one of the best weeks of my life as turned into a complete nightmare."

"I'd come to you if I could Mike," she stated. "I would like to help you thru this in any way I can."

"I'm glad to hear you say that Charlene because there is something you could help me with."

"And what's that?" she asked curiously.

Not precisely sure how to word my request and perhaps a bit tentative of her response, I asked "How about the Shield? Could the light frequency help him? Could it actually cure it?"

There was an immediate and hard silence. I could hear the slight sound of her breath in the receiver. A sudden streak of fear coursed thru my body as I was certain I had pushed the bounds of our friendship.

"Hello?" I said. "Are you still there?"

"Yes I am Mike. Sorry. It's just that I wasn't expecting this kind of request. It's not that simple."

Realizing the enormous pressure I had just extended to her, I tried to relinquish the appeal saying "If he can't go, it's ok. I just thought it might work."

"Let me see what I can do Mike. I can't say for sure but perhaps you and Mason can come here for a bit."

Not wanting to add any pressure or any further inconvenience on her I simply said "Ok, thanks. Let me know if you can make this happen."

"Ok Mike. I'll get back to you as soon as I can. Bye for now."

"Thanks Charlene," I replied. "Bye."

In the hastiness and nervousness of my request, I inadvertently forgot to ask if Jason could come as well. "Dam," I thought, "I wonder if that will be a problem?" Within twenty minutes, my little phone rang and with nervous optimism, I answered.

"Hi Mike. How do you feel?"

By the simply gleeful and cheerful tenor to her voice, I knew this was good news.

"Can I assume that you have good news for me Charlene?" I asked.

"Sure do Mike. It's all good. The both of you can be here within the next couple of days."

Thrilled with the idea that Mason was going to have a shot at obliterating this horrible disease which was attacking his young precious body, I couldn't help but feel the gavel coming down as it pertained to Jason.

Before I could request or even suggest if Jason could accompany us, Charlene blurted "Yeah, it's all good Mike. It took some arm twisting but Carl finally agreed on one guest."

At that point, I knew not to even mention Jason.

"Great" I said. "When will you send me the travel times?"

"I'll have them ready by the end of the day," she answered. "I'll fax them to you."

"I really can't wait to see you Mike," she continued. "It's only been a few days but it seems like forever."

"I'm looking forward to seeing you as well. Should I pack for an even longer duration?" I inquired.

A slight giggle escaped thru the phone as she said "Sure."

"See you soon Charlene."

"Ok bye Mike."

Making my way to Jason's while charged with zestful anticipation, there was still a note of skepticism lingering in my mind. I had no doubt that Jason would allow Mason to accompany me to the Shield. Cindy, however, was another story. The jury was still out on if she would allow it. With a sorrowful greeting and a customary condolences hugs and kisses out of the way, we sat around Jason and Cindy's circular marble top dining room table discussing the probabilities of a successful journey. As anticipated, Jason gave his ok and was thrilled at the prospect of the possibility of a positive prognosis for Mason. Needless to say Cindy was slightly more leery and a tad pessimistic about the outcome. While perhaps she could sense the determination within me or maybe the complete desperation stemming from Jason she soon agreed with the venture. Jason called Mason into the room and with three sets of teary eyes fixed on him he asked "What's wrong now?"

"Nothing Buddy," Jason said.

"You and Uncle Mikey are going to take a trip; a trip that will hopefully get rid of the trouble with your legs."

"Really Uncle Mike, really?" Mason said euphemistically.

"That's right May-May. You and me," I answered.

Stretching out my arms to embrace my godson, he walked towards me as if to reciprocate my actions then suddenly struck me hard on the right shoulder. "Gotcha Uncle Mike," he laughed.

"You little pecker," I yelped and we all broke out laughing.

Mason was remarkably calm seeing that this was his first time flying. A little, "ohhh" on take off and an "ahhh" as we touched down. I guess the excitement of my first trip was so extreme for I found myself almost accustomed to a private jumbo jet. There was a different feeling crossing the tarmac this time. The fighter jets, the heavily armed commandos were again present but for some reason, there was no tension. I guess I just knew what to expect this time. Mason however seemed to be absorbing every nuance like a sponge to water. Thinking it was strange to be proceeding by ourselves and wondering if I could remember how to enter the Shield, the door that led to the descending shaft opened and the beautiful shapely contour of Charlene appeared.

"I'm so glad to see you Mike," she said.

"It's good to be back," I replied as we embraced. Looking over my shoulder with our arms still entwined she said "You must be Mason."

"Hi. It's nice to meet you."

I recognized an immediate connection between them. I can't explain it, it was just there. Proceeding down the shaft thru the steel corridor and once again facing the large stainless steel door that led to paradise, I kept my focus on Mason and his reaction. Perhaps it would give me an idea of how Charlene, Carl and the others saw me when I first entered. As the grand door lifted and the unmistakable scent of jasmine refilled my nostrils, I couldn't help but have that feeling of coming home from a long trip even though this wasn't my home. Walking towards the crystal clear lake to our right, it was as if nothing had changed. I'm not certain if it was psychosomatic but I certainly and definitely felt stronger and healthier immediately. Charlene guided us past the arrangement of apple and peach trees which lined the left side of the walkway that led to the concrete structure where I had enjoyed the fantastic light show previously. Taking her lead, we entered the building.

"What are we doing in here Charlene?" I asked curiously.

"Just follow me guys. You'll understand in two seconds."

Walking hand in hand in hand, Charlene, Mason and I proceeded thru the dazzle of the light array. The beams bounced and jumped and seemed to encircle our entire bodies. Not knowing if we were walking straight or from side to side, we continued behind Charlene's lead.

"Uncle Mike," Mason uttered, as I could feel his grip tightening on my hand, but before I could answer him the lights suddenly stopped.

"What was that? Mason asked. I could sense the slightest tone of fear in his little voice. "Its ok buddy, it's ok," I repeated. "Charlene, what was that?"

"The lights were a scanning device," she answered. "Kind of like; what you would think of as an x-ray."

"An x-ray?" I repeated.

Looking directly towards me, she softly winked and said "Yeah, like an x-ray."

I quickly realized that Mason had just undergone a complete medical exam. "Quite clever," I thought to myself; conducting an obviously superior examination so soon to our arrival, alleviating all pressures and tensions.

"This way guys," Charlene ordered. Passing thru yet another steel door, we found ourselves in the midst of a huge compound. Hundreds of bamboo huts lined up into seven different rows all converging at the far end towards one larger hut. On the left side of the compound was again a buffet style dining hall where approximately fifty people were sitting, talking and leisurely dining on a wide variety of eateries. We strolled down the center isle that led us to the large hut. As we approached the door, it suddenly opened and out marched Carl.

"Good morning my dear, Mike and you must be Mason."

With a smile on my face and surrendering my hand, I said "Hi Carl. How are you?"

"Oh fine, fine," he replied. "I'm just about to get something to eat. Would you care to join me or would you rather see the results?"

"I think we'll go read the results before we do anything," Charlene said quickly.

"Certainly," Carl submitted. "See you in a bit."

Charlene once again taking the lead and entering the large facility, I stopped saying "Just a minute."

Running back to catch up to Carl, I stopped him and asked "Something wrong Carl? I can't put my finger on it but it seems that something is wrong."

"No, not at all," he replied.

"I want to thank you Carl for allowing Mason to come here. I really hope that the rejuvenating capabilities of the light frequency can help him."

"I understand Mike. I understand completely. Of course you realize, if it does work, it will only work here."

Pondering that very thought for a moment and understanding the diversity of its implication, I was subsequently stricken with the harsh reality of its validity. … What happens when we leave?

In a hasty retreat back towards Charlene and Mason, I could hear the echo of Carl saying "We'll work it out Mike." There was a definite concern painted on Mason's face as I approached him. Trying my best to hide my own fears, I smiled and said "Ok, let's go buddy." We followed Charlene thru a darkened hallway that had an eerie and uncanny atmosphere.

It wasn't until that exact point in time that I realized I had yet to see any writing. No signs, no pictures, no books, not so much as a clock on a wall. Time, it seemed, had no essence here. Coming from a place where a person's entire thought pattern was dictated by television, newspapers, billboards, hell, even clothing had its own subliminal message. I began to understand the simplicity of life here. It wasn't just the plain white garments that people wore, or the ordinary natural presentation of the women without make-up, jewelry or the pungent aroma of a hundred different perfumes. This entire society was consumed by individuality. I could hardly imagine three hundred unencumbered entities, each possessing their own interpretation of existence, without the slightest influence of forced abstract thought.

As Charlene, Mason and I entered a room which I presumed by the surrounding equipment was a medical facility, Charlene instructed Mason to prop himself up on the single rectangular stainless steel table which was situated in the centre of the room. The walls were adorned with what I could only describe as futuristic implements. Not knowing their use or their importance, I simply stood mystified. Charlene however, seemingly comfortable in this surrounding, took my hand and said "It should only take a minute" but before she could finish her sentence, Jennifer walked through the door.

"Hello again Mike," she said pleasantly.

Recognizing her from my initial encounter, I replied "Hello Jennifer, nice to see you again."

"Good to see you too Mike," she answered. "And hello Mason. My name is Jennifer. I'm the medical technician. I'm here to help you understand and treat your illness."

Unfolding a small hand held computer, about the size of a compact calculator, she began punching in a sequence of digits.

"Well," she said as she walked towards Mason, "it does seem as though there are complications in your nervous system." Upon hearing that, I gently placed my right arm around Mason's shoulder to try to comfort him and to reassure him of my presence.

"So what can we do to fix this?" I asked.

"Quite frankly Mike," Jennifer responded "the degenerative state is already remissive. I think with seven to ten days of ultra light therapy, there would be no residue of imperfections in his system."

"You mean he will be totally cured?"

"Not exactly Mike," she answered. "Mason's genetic make-up is prone for this imbalance. While he is here, the distinct light frequency will compensate and refurbish his system with regenerating profiles. However, if he should leave here, his original chemical imbalance would re-emerge, facilitating the same manifestations of that crippling disorder."

Elated yes upon hearing her diagnosis and realizing the extreme fortune of his recovery, I still moreover swayed with the realization of the enormous and most difficult task that lay ahead… simply informing Jason and Cindy that their little boy may not be able to come home. Of course there was the distinct possibility that Cindy would object to the relocation of her only son but I honestly believed Jason could convince her of the benefit.

Shortly proceeding Jennifer's opinion and with tentative optimism, I gently struck Mason on his right shoulder and asked "you feel like some grub?"

The calming measure seemed successful as he chuckled back "yep!"

I thanked Jennifer for her expertise while Charlene, sensing the urgency and need for a new surrounding, gestured the same. With the resumption of small talk as we walked hastily back towards the main food court, my thoughts reverted into a new topic. No longer consumed with anxiety about Mason's condition, I began picturing a serene and romantic image of Charlene and I. "Really good soup hey Uncle Mike ….."

"What, what was that Mason?"

Chapter 14

"I don't know all the details. It's not like we have a choice. What are you saying? You don't trust Mike?"

"That's not what I'm saying Jason," Cindy jolted.

"Well, that's what it sounded like to me," Jason barked. "Maybe if you didn't…"

"Didn't what Jason? Didn't what?" as her voice began to crack.

"You know God dam well what," Jason snapped. "I'm sure all that stupid wine with diner and wine with supper had some kind of effect or probably is why he has what he has."

Swiftly raising her right hand and thrusting it against his left cheek she screamed "you son of a bitch!" and stomped out of the bedroom, slamming the door behind her.

With the cling of the doorbell, Jason collected himself and calmly walked to the door still feeling the sting and heat that lingered on his cheek. Standing on the opposite side were two well-groomed clean shaven men in military attire. The tall fellow stood six foot four with wide bulging shoulders. His black hair trimmed tight, his deep brown self-assured eyes glared forward without expression. The other while not as tall was slightly denser. He had blonde hair that slightly peered out of the rim of his cap. However, the hardness in his rugged blue eyes stood firm.

"Yes, can I help you?" Jason asked timidly.

"Mr. Tanndy," the tall gentleman said. "I'm Colonel Patrick St-Jean, US Army. This is Major Rodregus. We have a few questions regarding the death of Mr. Steve Markinson. May we come in?" he asked.

"Certainly, come on in," Jason replied. Jason led them to the sitting room which overlooked his beautifully landscaped backyard. "Please have a seat," he suggested. "Can I get you anything?"

"No thank you Mr. Tanndy," Colonel Patrick replied as they both took their seats.

Obviously curious and perhaps a bit anxious as to why the US Army had an involvement in the investigation of Steve's death, Jason shrugged his shoulders and opened both his palms upwards and asked "So, what's this about?"

"We understand that you had access via the code to the security system of Mr. Markinson's dwelling," Colonel Patrick stated.

"That's right," Jason replied. "Mike and I both knew the security code."

"Why?" Jason asked curiously.

Major Rodregis, automatically broke in asking "To your knowledge, is there anyone else that had that code?"

"No." Jason said, "Just Mike and I, why does it mean anything?"

"Are you sure?" Colonel Patrick reiterated. "Are you absolutely positive nobody else had that code?"

"Yes, I'm positive," Jason replied.

Quickly glancing to one another, the two army men stood up abruptly and nodded saying "Thank you. That will be all."

Jason, a bit dumbfounded asked once again "What's all this about. I thought the police said this was an accident. What's going on?"

"We are not at liberty to discuss this any further," Colonel Patrick blurted "but we will inform you if circumstances permit."

Sharply marching back towards the front door, Major Richard turned and asked "So, you are sure?"

"Yes I am" Jason replied. "I'm sure."

Whispering to himself while closing the door behind them, he muttered "What the hell is going on?"

Trotting back thru his lavishly decorated living room, Jason stopped to admire the picture of the three amigos that hung over the mantel of the marble laced crowned fireplace. He quickly conjured up the event and memories of the precise moment that capsulated the three smiling faces in the portrait. It was the day they had opened their first Maymoo Tech building; long before the vast wealth and prestige of society; a time when the uncertainty and excitement of big business was still yet a mystery.

Perhaps in his own way, Jason longed for a simpler and more intimate rapport with Steve and me. The men we had become were not indicative of the men we were. Standing there mesmerized, Cindy approached him from behind. Sensing her presence, he reached behind him and rubbed his right hand across her belly.

"I'm sorry Baby," he spoke low and apologetically. "I'm really sorry."

Raising both her hands to rest gently on each of his shoulders, she responded "I know, Honey. I know." "I heard what you were talking about. What does the army have to do with Steve?"

"I'm not sure Cin. I'm not sure about a lot of things."

"You don't think that they think you had something to do with Steve's death, do you?"

A sudden chill raced up Jason's long muscular frame as he turned towards his wife in a submissive and fearful shrug saying "Oh my God! You think?"

With a perplexed grimace painted on both their faces, they quickly surmised the possibility that Steve's accident could possibly not be an accident.

While retreating in separate directions, Cindy all dressed to the nines, skipped out the front door and into her sky blue STS Cadillac and drove off. Jason meanwhile, scampered downstairs into his den and feverishly began sorting thru files. As a few restless hours passed and Jason having his nose buried deep into his work, the ringing of the phone broke the concentrated silence. Jason raised his eyebrows peering slightly over the crest of his laptop as his eyes focused in on the intruding sound of the phone.

"Hello," Jason answered.

"Jay-man! It's Mike. How's it going?"

"Damn Mike. I'm not sure. Really, I don't know. How are things going with Mason? With all the shit going on here right now, I could use some good news."

"The news is Buddy - all good. My friends tell me that Mason can make a 100% recovery here with absolutely no trace or hindrance of MD."

"That's fantastic Buddy. It's just what I needed to hear right now. I mean that's just great!"

Yah, I knew you'd be happy Jay. I almost jumped out of my skin when I found out myself. So how are things going up there anyway?"

"Funny you should ask Mike" Jason replied. "I had a major weird visit today!"

"Really" I asked inquisitively. "From whom?"

"Two men from United States Army came around asking questions about Steve's security code. They wanted to know how many people knew the code."

"How many people knew the code?" I asked.

"Yeh, how many people knew the code. I mean has far as I know" Jason continued, "We are the only ones other than himself that knew it."

"Is there anyone that you know that had the code?"

"Hell no," I replied. "You know how he was with his security."

"Yah, I know," Jason concluded.

"What else did they ask you?"

"That was it," Jason said. "I was thinking," Jason remarked "do you remember last year when Steve went to Charlotte, North Carolina for three days?"

"Yah: what about it?" I answered.

"Well, it may not mean anything but you know how he was. Anytime he went some place or did something, we all had to hear about it. But when he returned from North Carolina, he didn't want to discuss the trip at all."

"That's true," I said. "So, what are you thinking?"

"Nothing really," Jason replied. "But isn't there a huge army base in Charlotte?"

"To tell you the truth Jason, I don't really know but I'll sure as shit find out." As a tense clearing chuckle fluttered across the line, I knew my call had alleviated an enormous weight off of Jason's shoulders.

"So when do you think you guys will be back?" Jason asked.

"A couple of days," I told him even though I wasn't completely sure myself.

"All right, I guess I'll talk to you when you get back. See you later Mike."

"Talk to you soon," I said.

Chapter 15

After lunch, Charlene explained how she had a few duties to perform and she suggested that Mason and I roam freely about the Shield so that we may familiarize ourselves with all its surroundings. And as she suggested, we did.

Mason and I canoed across the crystal clear lake, walked thru the bountiful assortment of fruit trees that stood scattered throughout the orchard. The variety of fresh fruit was only outmatched by the ample supply of garden eateries. We also made a stop at the fishery where four individuals took pleasure in the activity of feeding, cleaning and harvesting fresh fish for the next meal's menu. Even though Mason was accustomed to having pretty much everything he ever desired I could see the contentment in his eyes as we scurried around the Shield. It was as if he was meant to be here. Not that he was lazy or thoughtless but he genuinely seemed to be enjoying this place. He took advantage at every opportune moment to delight in conversation with passers by, absorbing the pleasantries and camaraderie of all the individuals we encountered.

To convey a tangible understanding of the atmosphere, it is like a family reunion with the exhilaration and excitement of meeting long lost cherished acquaintances. I've known Mason all his life and certainly had a great influence on his upbringing however I began to sense even in that short period of time his individualism and independence breaking thru. Of course I had the admiration and glee like that of a proud father so to speak. To see him interact and converse in such an intelligible and grown up fashion induced a slight sense of jealousy lingering on my palate. It just seemed he was slipping away minute by minute here. Perhaps, I thought to myself this was yet just another side effect of this place or maybe a defining trait of the metaphysical changes he was developing.

After a few hours of indulgence, we found ourselves loitering around a palm tree making casual conversation with one of the residents. Her name was Diane. She was a medium build brown haired beauty. Her seductive red lips failed only in comparison to her deep lustful brown eyes. Her long feathered and tapered cut hair draped slightly off her shoulders. Even though she wore a traditional robe which was indicative of the attire, it was easy to see her curvaceous and well developed body cascading thru the mundane robe… quite revealing. That is to say, she stuck out in all the right places. Diane told us of the extreme and harsh outer life she had experienced growing up on the streets of Glenfin, Scotland. She re-counted her troublesome and impoverished upbringing and in a remorseful commemoration denounced her own family for not providing a more suitable or desirable childhood. Her story of an alcoholic father and a viperous trifling trollop of a tramp for a mother certainly had taken its toll on the young sultriest. While verbally re-enacting her encounter with the perverse and diabolical callers which roamed the one bedroom flat that she called her abode. She described the scene as nothing less than a tragic and pitiful emancipation of existence. The trouble in her beautiful brown eyes soon gave way to that of extreme joyfulness and happiness as she explained how Carl and Jennifer picked her out from her desolate and deplorable surroundings and invited her to the new Eden. Never in her wildest dreams could she even imagine or hope to imagine a life so serene and enjoyable. She made mention however, in a strange and obscure way that there was a price to be paid for her blissful and bountiful surroundings but before she could specify as to the particular cost, we interrupted by the voice of Charlene saying "I thought I'd find you guys here." As if ordered with a silent command, Diane swiftly turned and began walking away. "Rather odd," I thought to myself as a lingering curiosity remained tumbling in my mind of what price Diane had paid for her resurrection of life.

While brisk fully walking along the seemingly endless barrage of onlookers that appeared to take great interest in our direction, Charlene inquired as to the status of our weariness asking "What do you say we catch a nap?"

Feeling a tad peaked, I agreed wholeheartedly.

"We've prepared a hut for both of you. I hope it's to your liking."

Within a few hundred meters, we found ourselves at the entrance of one of the larger bamboo huts.

"This one's yours Mike," she said. "Mason, yours is on the other side."

While I watched Mason as he marched up to his own hut, he gave me a subtle glance over his right shoulder and confidently entered. With fatigue setting in, I dredged my way into my own hut. It was very basic to say the least. A single rod of illumination hung from the eight foot ceiling. There was absolutely nothing draping from the coarse, rough lined walls. Approximately fifteen by fifteen feet, the only two articles in the room were a tiny nightstand that resembled marble and a single sized bed draped with a fluffy white blanket. I could only assume that these were the normal accommodations prepared for guests, judging from the atmosphere of the Shield it made total sense. That is to say these were people motivated by much more that the acclimation of positions or tenure. During my brief scan of my newly acquired lodging my thoughts could hardly fine time to rest, with so much uncertainty an anxiety within the course of a day I was abandoned by my own capability for abstract thought. I decided to lie down and try to put some perspective towards the events of the day when the door to my hut suddenly and surprisingly opened.

"Yes," I said curiously.

"It's just me Mike," the voice said.

The subtle sultry sound of Charlene's beckon was easily picked up from my wiry yet excited ears.

Suddenly fatigue swiftly receded and excitement took its place. I was instantly infused with a new vigor. The mere site of Charlene's silhouette sent a rush of sensual sensation coursing to my loins. Without another word and to my total amazement, she began discarding the simple robe which covered her beautifully and sensuous well-proportioned body. Like a child standing in front of a Christmas tree loaded with presents beneath it, I could only stare and watch as she tiptoed towards me with her now radiantly naked body. Simply gesturing with a slight flick of her hand for me to push over, she innocently lay down beside me. Curling up in the fetal position, she reached for the white blanket ensuring that we are both covered. Nestling her body tight to mine, she said "Get some sleep Mike."

Chapter 16

"Skyhawk, skyhawk…..please come in, my instruments have all gone down I'm flying blind….skyhawk, skyhawk do you copy over? Vector 6.44 bearing 318. Do you copy over…skyhawk, skyha…………."

"General Cobbs: the Statcam from the ICBU shows the same pattern from exactly the same coordinates. 6:44 bearing 318. They also confirm what we feared."

"That's not what I wanted to hear Colonel," the General bellowed. "That makes 16 aircrafts and submersibles we have lost in the 22 years I've been overseeing this phenomena."

"Yes general," Colonel St. Jean replied.

"It's just as if they disappeared off the face of the earth."

"Sir have we learned anything more about the incident regarding Steve Markinson?" the young and eager Major Richard Fortin asked.

"Anything more as to what?" the General barked.

With a now stern and disgruntled grimace on his face, General Cobbs peered directly at the young major who now regretted his once eager desire to join the conversation.

"What I meant to say General," the Major said but before he could finish his sentence the General turned his back towards him and shouted "This is unfucken acceptable." "I want some answers and I want them quick!" The 2 officers could easily see the vein popping out of the back of the General's neck. They knew full well the general was about to have a conniption.

"The last link we had in the past 3 years was that which we had acquired from Mr. Markinson. I find it very hard to accept that on the night before he was to give us the full disclosure on his development, he gets himself killed in a freak accident." "I've had it up to here with all this Bermuda Triangle bullshit, for three months our flybys have shown there is a deliberate jarring of the electrical and guidance systems as soon as a fighter or navel vessel enters those quadrates. This has gone on long enough, I'm ordering a fleet of six destroyers, 5 aircraft carriers and 24 search and rescue vessels to assemble and be ready to move by 0630 tomorrow, have your men ready on standby to facilitate this order…..and gentlemen, make no mistake about it we are going to get to the bottom of this by order of the president".

While Colonel St. Jean set out to follow the general's orders, he began to think back to the last meeting he had with Steve Markinson. He remembered the conversation when Steve had mentioned that the stuff he was involved with was going to change the world and just might be the most significant discovery possible. Even though Steve didn't give any other information about his findings, Mr. St Jean was confident and certainly convinced of its accuracy. The only clue he had left him with the bearing 644 by 318…..oddly enough the same bearing that was for the last 20 years the main area of missing and otherwise lost aircraft and navy vessels. There had to be a link to the two he thought…but what…maybe, just maybe there was a lot more to this phenomena then anybody knew. He knew however the general was indeed going to get to the bottom of it.

By 0600 the next morning, the entire fleet had been ordered to depart. The apprehension and fear which coursed thru the very core of the men and women serving on those vessels was exceedingly apparent. It wasn't as if it was abnormal for them to be shaken out of their racks and put thru the rigors of a training session so early in the morning, however they all knew that this was no training exercise. Moreover, it would be quite unusual for the navy to go thru such an ordeal just to check the readiness of a crew. Something serious was afoot and they all knew it.

"Inner calms are linked up Sir. You can address the fleet whenever you are ready Sir."

"Attention all decks. This is General Cobbs. We are about to embark on a most unusual and yet necessary campaign. As you are well aware, we have all lost friends and shipmates to this so called devil's triangle phenomena. It is never acceptable for the United States military to lose one of its own without an understanding, an explanation as to why, where, what and how. The President has mandated this as a priority one. We can no longer deny or ignore the fact that this area holds secrets that must be understood and accounted for. It is our job people to ensure the safety of our nation and those of our allies to not be impeded by this ……….. Whatever it is? I know you will all do your duty, and rest assured we will find the answers to these questions."

"Captain Dunns, make way," the General ordered.

Chapter 17

Once waking, I could hardly remember a better night's sleep. The comfort level of this little cot like bed was that of a fluffy, bulbous cloud. Even though I truly didn't have a clue as to the time of day, I was totally rested and full of energy. Charlene still laying silent beside me and arched in the fetal position, was as stunning as she was the night before. Humorous I thought; that funky smell of twisting and turning, mixed in with the sweet aroma of a woman's natural morning scent was absent. It was as if she had gotten up showered and returned to bed, not so much as a hair out of place. The events of the night before still fresh in my mind, the fact that we just laid there buck naked and never did the nasty. It wasn't as though I was expecting her to be all over me like a hornet from hell however the rejoinder she did give me was confusing to say the least. Watching her lay there I started thinking that perhaps she wanted to test my resolve, maybe she wanted to see if I was so preoccupied with sex that I would jump at the chance to pounce her bones. Don't get me wrong, that very idea did find itself circling the bowels of my mind, never the less I didn't or wouldn't take the chance of insulting or degrading her. It is a curious thing mind you, even though it had been to that point a long time since I had the gratification of the fairer sex, I hadn't, shall we say, received the go ahead from my main partner in that area. A shocking and even more disturbing thought soon came to me……no that couldn't be, not at my age but what was I to think, here was this beautiful sexy woman just laying there beside me. My god has that really happened could that be probable, here, now just when I meet the girl of my dreams? This would be the ultimate case of a shitty twist of fate however before I could linger into more self pity, the flap to my little abode flew open and a frenzied Carl rushed in saying.

"Sorry for the intrusion, but we have need of Charlene immediately!"

The once sleeping beauty sprang up like a panther and in one fluid motion darted and flipped on her robe.

"What's the quandary here Carl?" She asked in complete surprise.

"It seems we have to submerge to the bottom for a spell," he answered.

"Right to the bottom?" she questioned.

"I'm afraid so," he answered.

"Is there something you want to tell me here Carl?" I asked with extreme concern.

"Not at the moment Mike, there's no time to elucidate," he said.

All though I didn't know these people very long, I could tell there was something very wrong happening. It wasn't just the abrupt manner in which Carl entered the hut…although that was outlandish in it's self, but the look he gave Charlene was as if to say hasten we are in very deep. I dressed as rapidly as I could and rushed out of the hut to make my way to Mason's hut. There we're people running in all directions all around me. What once was a calm quiet place now seemed to be complete and total chaos.

Like ants running to attack a caterpillar that just invaded their living space they looked confused and disoriented however in the mist of all the turmoil I did start to notice a pattern emerging from within the craziness. Before I could make any sense of it all I felt a rumble a shake a thrusting downward sensation. The whole complex came to a halt. They stopped and looked at each other smiling as if to say its ok we made it. There was a pressure I could feel building up in my ears, the kind of feeling you get when you dive deep into the water, I immediately became I bit disoriented and a tad dizzy.

Within three minutes or so once again I felt a rumble, this time coming from directly beneath me. As I watched the others slowly regain there normal carefree persona I was left in a state of complete and utter distress. I was suddenly aware that this place was not only secluded from the eye of protection I enjoyed from the good old United States of America, but was out of the reach of anyone or anything. I didn't have to ask what had just happened I knew, somehow I just knew.

My next encounter was once again with Carl who had just stuck his head out of the main terminal. He casually walked up to me and as if nothing even took place saying.

"Hey Mike old boy, what's new?"

"What's new, what's new, I'll tell you what's new, I want to get the hell out of here that's what's new!" I shouted.

"Relax my friend relax you're just a bit shaken up over what happened is all. It's all good now," he explained in a reassuring tone.

"All good, all good, how the hell can you call all of this good, what happened," I demanded.

"Look Mike," he said, "there are things that go on here that you just couldn't possibly appreciate, and what's more I don't think I could even explicate clearly. You're just going to have to trust me for now ok."

"No it's not ok Carl I think I would like to leave and just go about my merry way if it's all the same to you. I thank you for the hospitality and the wondrous little world you've shown me but really I think I've seen and heard enough."

"You're not looking at the big picture here Mike. There is a whole other life that could be yours if you are just a little more patient."

"Look!" I said, "I'm not obtuse! I know the way I thought the world was is not really the way it is. It would take a complete moron not to figure out that you guys down, up, over, beside, whatever or wherever we are, really are in charge as far as the goings on in the world. But I can tell you this, even the best kept secret gets exposed."

"You could be right Mike, and you probably are, and as for being in charge of the goings on in the world, we really have no control of it. Really life outside the Shield is none of our concern," he continued. "The only tribulation we see as a community is that of the sufferings and the evil that we allow to continue up in your world!"

"Allow, isn't that just a bit too much a god like idealism to be floating around here Carl, I mean you're not gods are you? It's not as if you have the power to take over the whole planet is it?"

"Mike, I think you're letting your emotions get the better of you, after all, haven't I let your godson come here and get treated for his infirmity. What will happen if you'd go back home? Mason would have to suffer the riggers of a debilitating disease, not to mention the mental anguish of knowing that he could be healthy and pain free void of restrictions."

"What are you saying Carl, you would use your healing power here to trap us here?"

"Of course not Mike, you are free to leave anytime you like. I would never do something like that. It's just that you can't leave right this minute."

"And why's that?" I asked angrily.

"Well, it's like this. Right now we are seated at the very bottom of the Atlantic Ocean. There are at this very second, thirty or so navel vessels approaching this very point. That is to say seven thousand meters up. I'm certain you've heard the mystery surrounding the Bermuda Triangle. Well now you discern the answer. There is no mystery. The magnetic resonator sends out a certain field distortion that makes it impossible for the electronic key pads of any vessel to guide its way through this field. Of course there were times that some ships and air craft came into visual site of our island, and regrettably we had to destroy them. Not that it gave us gratification in any way, but it was necessary to protect ourselves from the rest of humanity which as you know is not very humane at all. Nevertheless about two hours ago our radar singled out a massive infiltration to this position, rather than sink thirty ships it was better to just descend our island to the bottom of the ocean. It doesn't happen too often maybe three or four times a year and it will stimulate our family a bit. That's why everyone got a little crazy. You may have found that you felt a little light headed, or even dizzy, that's because the resonator was putting out massive amounts of electro magnetic beams in order to scramble the instrumentation of the oncoming ships. Losing your equilibrium was just a momentary side affect. Once the convoy passes by and there is no jeopardy in raising to the surface you will be able to leave Mike, no one is holding you hostage. Besides we could reside down here for ten years if need be."

I couldn't believe the shit I was hearing, not only was he telling me that we were sitting at the bottom of the ocean, and that the Shield was responsible for the deaths of hundreds if not thousands of innocent people. I believe he was trying to convey that there was no reprieve in near site for my return to my conventional world. Before I had a chance to tell him of the complete fucking asshole I thought he and the rest of this clan was, Mason ran up to me and said, "Uncle Mike isn't this just the best ever or what, that was the coolest thing I ever seen!"

"Mason," I said "You don't understand what's going on here!"

"Sure I do Uncle Mike, Jennifer told me all about it last night, and I think it's pretty neat don't you?"

Not knowing how to respond to his question, I simply nodded. The last thing I wanted to do was to get Mason involved in my disapproval of the Shield. Besides, I got the feeling from Carl that it would not be such a daunting task to liberate them of us if he saw fit. So I thought the best thing to do was to play it a bit cooler, perhaps Carl would take my unfavorable words earlier as just that from a anxious man………. perhaps not!

MEANWHILE ON THE SURFACE…………………….

"I don't understand it General, it was right here! Radar, print out the last area contacts before the board went crazy."

"Yes sir." The enthusiastic young bridge officer replied.

Staring out the window with his arms stiffly at his side and his hands clasped sternly to his back, general Cobbs peered relentlessly through the main view window. Not a word was spoken by the crew who by now knew that it was in their best interest not to make the slightest sound as not to disturb the general's thoughts. All though there were eight individuals standing in relatively close proximity the silence stood heavy with the expectation of the generals impending explosion. The only reverberation echoing the room was the Tap. Tap. Tap of the printer spelling out the answer that would facilitate the general's anger. None of the bridge officers were too prompt to retrieve the printout once the noise of the printer had come to its conclusion. Looking around the diminutive room as if to say "I'm not getting it" they all took there turn at measuring up who would have the unpleasant task of handing the document to general Cobbs. Finally captain St. Jean standing strong and confident walked over to the computer consul and retrieve the answer the rest of the crew were so adamantly trying to avoid.

With a brief glance downward, they could see the slightest slug appear on those massive wide shoulders of his; never the less he ripped the paper from the machine and headed directly over to the general. As he stretched out his long powerful arm to extend to the general the paper that he knew was going to infuriate him, captain St. Jean tried desperately to defuse the situation by asking, "Do you really need to see this sir?"

With a momentary pause, the general gradually turned to face the other officers in the group and simply said "I suppose not Captain. Just start a system wide system failure check. Report our findings with those of the rest of the fleet and have a briefing set up for 0700."

While relieved by the calm reaction the general expressed, captain St. Jean knew full well the implication of the moment. This wasn't the time or the place to blow up, but he also had the feeling the proverbial shit was certainly going to hit the fan…… along with a few other choice articles.

Reinvigorated by Captain St. Jean's tactics, the bridge swiftly began the hustle and bustle of caring out the general's orders. Data from the 45 ships making up the convoy came in with a steady pace. The F14's downloaded their scanner makers, not a single jet recorded the same findings. When all the pieces were put together and every single solitary line of data was collected, captain St. Jean headed down to the central command area to present his findings and that of the entire fleet to general Cobbs. As he reached the outer door to the conference room he couldn't help notice the general pacing back and forth. Reflecting on the state of the general's earlier measure of patience, he braced himself for the out pouring of hostility and down right angers the general was going to unleash, after all; he was now only addressing the senior officers and it wasn't like him to hold back in that kind of atmosphere.

He wasn't a timid man "Captain St. Jean." By any account moreover he had proven himself as a dam straight hero on two separate occasions. He once pulled three injured men out of a burning helicopter in a freak exercise accident. The other commendation was given to him by the president himself for valor. Under heavy enemy fire he single handedly charged across a mine field in the Iranian conflict, to reacquire the communication pack that was inadvertently left behind when the entire platoon had to bail on a position that left them stranded in the wide open, Needing to call for air support the then "lieutenant St. Jean." Staggered and swerved thru gun fire and successfully called in the coordinates to facilitate a much needed air strike. By all accounts he was a genuine all American hero. All that being understood, he still wasn't relishing the thought of having to bring the general such bad news, after all he had seen the generals mean side in more ways than one. No he was just plain nervous to tell "uncle Cobbs."

"So what happened out here today, captain?" Cobbs demanded.

"Well sir from all the data we have, it seems as though there was an object 6000 meters long by 2400 meters wide straight a stern six and half miles out. The density can only be categorized as being a solid mass, that is to say an island. For some and to this point unknown reason, the second our fog radar was initiated all com-terminals' just aborted their course and scrambled to an unknown frequency. As you well know when there is any discrepancy in our ship's auto command the computer shuts down all power to the engines and awaits new vector programming. The scrambling of the data on our surface fleet as well as that air born lasted for 3 minutes and fourteen seconds. When we reacquired interface with the main computers the data seemed to almost disappear, there were only small fragments of information remaining in the memory banks. Of those that we could decipher, it looks as though just seconds before the anomaly disappears, a small area approximately three hundred square yards was clearly visible. From the recording of the aerial shot taken by eagle "Iron side", we can confirm that indeed there was solid earth momentarily. Again we can offer up no explanation as to how or why this solid mass disappeared; only the fact that it was there and then it wasn't. General I think we must assume that there is a certain and definite ulterior power at works here!"

There certainly was a look of shock bestowed upon every face in the room. Undoubtedly and understandably, a new circumstance that the armed forces had never come across before was about to be realized. Sure its one thing to go into battle with other armies whiles all the time knowing one has an imputable force. But entering into the complete unknown was unnerving to say the least. Not even general Cobbs with his vast military experience were beyond concern. The possibility that they were facing a new or even more advance adversary seemed remote however one could not put aside the development of the last twenty-four hours and not feel inferior. While the others searched each others faces for understanding and an explanation to this dilemma, general Cobbs hesitantly picked up the red telephone that sat directly in front of him and in a raspy type voice said………"I need to speak with the president immediately!"

Chapter 18

Seeming like an eternity since Mike and Mason took off for their fun filled journey cascading through the wonderment of what must have been heaven, Jason and Cindy found it quite difficult to resume to their everyday routine. Jason took time off of work; which was by no means a habitual thing. He was the first to show up each and every morning, and most often the very last person to leave. Cindy had stopped going to her work out sessions, and the hair salon like she had been doing for the preceding fifteen years. They didn't realize it but without their son around to take to ball practice, or football or even to cook for, they both had a rigid time to fill in time. Life just seemed to be dredging on. They both found the days and especially the nights too long to cover. Keeping busy was never a quandary before, but now it was the greatest challenge they faced on a daily basis. Even if an encounter under the covers was called for and long over due, it seemed to end up in a fight. To put it mildly they were both in a desperate way.

It's easy to understand the predicament they faced; it must have been so grueling for them to not only have to deal with a sick son, but to have the courage to allow him to trek so far away in the mere hope of a cure. Looking back now I think of the stress my two friends must have endured it always leaves me puzzled .When I'm forced to ask myself if I could do the same, it invariably comes out no.

"Say Cindy, I've been thinking; it's not like were doing ourselves any good just sitting around the house waiting on tenterhooks to hear from Mason. Why don't we bundle a few bags and head off to Vegas, we can network the house phone to our cell and just get away from here for a bit. I don't know about you but if things keep up this way I'm almost certain to end up in the loony- bin."

In the first loving ambiance Jason heard in the last two weeks, and just in the nick of time might I add, Cindy said, "Hey that really sounds like a refreshing proposal jay."

While packing their cases Cindy just happened to bend over the couch reaching out to pick up a silk flowered patterned scarf. Jason just happened to be looking at her at the time and well you could imagine the encounter the two of them had; after all it was weeks of harsh times, unknowing circumstances, not to mention the tension that seemed to circumnavigate them twenty four hours a day. They made love that afternoon, not normal husband and wife love; rather the kind of love making one finds with a stranger, or the loving after a huge fight, you know the kind of hard, relentless, angry love.

Jason and Cindy always shared a deep bonded kind of love; I was never the sort to believe in something as corny like "I found my soul mate" or "this is our destiny", that all seemed just a bit too unrealistic in my view. I guess not having my mother around to extend the unselfish, unequivocal type of love only a mother could provide, left me a shade barren and lacking in that department. However; as it pertained to them, Jason & Cindy, that sort of unblemished, devoted, self-sacrificing love did exist. Last fall; while Steve, Jason, and I were on our annual trip to Mud Lake, Jason out of the blue asked us if we thought that love and marriage was a fifty/fifty deal? Steve wasn't married but he was still with Ann; they never thought it necessary to walk down the isle. I think they both loved each other enough, but like to live by themselves. For myself, well I didn't trust or even have any inclination of marriage, so the only reference I could conger up was that of the talk shows and the way everyone thinks men and women are equal. It's not like I didn't think we were equal I just never pondered that thought before. Anyway; he asked if we thought love and marriage was fifty/fifty. Steve and I both agreed that yes, certainly love and marriage had to be fifty/fifty in order for things to run smoothly in a household. While thinking we came up with the correct answer, Jason floored the both of us when he said "no it isn't fifty/fifty…..its one hundred percent/nothing. Here we were thinking those two had a perfect marriage, and all the while Jason was trapped in a loveless vicious cycle of all give and no take. I tried to console him by telling him to keep his head up, and not to forget he had a beautiful son that thought the world of him. Then he started to chuckle and said the strangest thing to us:

"No boys, I give one hundred percent all the time, and expect nothing in return. Its then and only then when your giving is reciprocated…….. that you're in a truly loving home. If you're expecting to get love when you give love, well then isn't that just giving what you get? But my friends if you give it your all and don't expect her all, the love that she does lavish on you is from the heart and absolutely real."

Steve and I sat there dumbfounded with our mouths wide opened, once thinking that our good buddy was hurting and living a life of pure hell, all the time it was just as we thought…….he was the luckiest son-of-a-bitch on the planet. I guess the old adage is true. Behind every successful man stands a good woman. It was just the motivation that had permitted me to pursue the feelings, and the immediate bond that seemed evident with my initial sighting of Charlene. I longed for the emotional closeness that Jason had with his wife. I thought that perhaps the gods of love saw fit to endow and bestow upon me the same type of happiness. Naïve, Maybe; worth the chance, definitely! If the result of putting forth a genuine effort was only half of what Jason & Cindy shared….. Then the benefits' far outweighed the cost.

With that freshly laid face appearance, Jason was busy loading the car with their bags as Cindy took that time to do some last minute beautifying in the foyer mirror. Shutting the trunk of his shiny new metallic blue Bentley, he turned and found himself face to face with Ann. She was standing there holding a suitcase in her hands. Not sure as to what to ruminate, he asked.

"Going somewhere Ann?"

She immediately broke out crying collapsing into Jason's chest.

"What's the matter Ann? Are you ok? What happened?"

Sobbing and clinching on to him she could barely make out the words she was trying desperately to conger up.

"I was coming back from my mother's; I just had to get away after the accident, when I got to my driveway I could see the silhouette of two men standing in my living room. I was so terrified I just didn't know where to turn. I tried to go to Mike's house but no-one was there. I'm sorry; if you don't want me to be here I'll leave."

"Don't be ridiculous, you know you're always welcome here at any time, your family Ann you know that!"

"Thanks Jay, I'm just so frightened; who do you think is in my house? And why?"

"I don't know honey, but I promise to find out. Go in the house and tell Cindy what you just told me, I'll be back as soon as I can!"

Spinning his tires as he fled his driveway, Jason drove directly to Mickey's house. Mickey just happened to be the biggest mother we knew. Not like we hung out with him, but on occasion we would buy his services for shall we say peace keeping duty? If the boys and I were going out on the town with the girls, and we sought to ensure it was trouble free....Mickey was our man. This guy was six foot nine and weighed a whooping 395 pounds. There's a narrative around town that he hit this guy just for bumping into him; and sent his jaw three quarters of the way thru his skull. Needless to say did no one mess with Mickey! When Jason arrived at the big man's house, he knocked on the door and as usual Mickey answered in his pajamas.

"Hey Mr. Tanndy, what are you doing here?"

"I need your help Mickey, I need it badly!" Jason told him.

"You got it dude!" He replied.

"I need you now Mickey; right now!"

"I'll change!" He said.

It was an unmitigated relief to Jason that number one; Mickey was home, and number two he was disposed to help out without even knowing what he was heading into: I guess when you're that big there's not too much you have to fret about. But still; Jason felt a prompt release of nervousness' abandon him. Looking throughout the dingy little house, it was quite apparent that Mickey needs were not too extravagant. The old and out dated furniture reminded Jason of just how lucky he was. The stench that emanated out the room made his stomach turn. This certainly must have been the last place Jason would want to be, but as it were; the only place he could.

"So what's the trouble Mr. Tanndy?" Mickey inquired.

"I have a friend who found a couple of guys in her house this afternoon. Needless to say she's overwhelmed by the whole thing and asked me for help. That's where you come in."

"Hey I understand. No problem, just point the way."

"I'm not looking for you to knock the shit out of them. I need them to be able to talk. I want to find out why and what and for who they are working for!"

"You got it boss," he replied.

"Look, this could be nothing it could be something. I want you knowing that going in."

"Like I said boss, don't worry, it's not like this is my first … Mission!"

His relaxed attitude kind of gave Jason a bit more contentment. He never had any experience in this sort of thing however he was now convinced his partner in crime had profusion. Driving over to Ann's place they rehearsed the strategy that would have the best chance at success. Jason would go thru the front door; while big Mickey entered thru the back. Having the key ensured that Mickey could enter with out notice, and be able to help Jason should the need arise. Jason took a deep breath then knocked on the door. He waited a minute then using the spare key in the mail box he unlocked it and walked in. The two men were still there sitting at the small round kitchen table.

"Oh, I wasn't aware that Ann had asked someone else to stop in from time to time, and you are?" He asked calmly and politely.

"Just a friend." The skinny short blond hair man said as he looked over to his rather large husky, scarred face friend.

"Well I'm not sure why you're here, but I find it a bit peculiar that the door was locked and you didn't even answer when I knocked."

The two intruders looked Jason up and down sizing him up as it were; deciding he was no kind of threat, shrugged their shoulders as the big guy said.

"So what's it to you?"

My guess is they were about to put a real beating on him, right up till the point that Mickey stepped out from behind the hallway wall and replied.

"Cause we want to know!"

The intimidating, disrespecting manner they addressed Jason mere seconds before was most certainly causing the two hooligans deep regrettable anguish, easily read by their dropping faces when they saw the enormous monster accompanying the little wimpy Jason. Mickey swiftly darted between the two strangers and Jason. It's hard to believe a man that size could move so fast; startling Jason as well in the process. They both knew their next move was going to be their testimony to life. Jason; now brimming with absolute and total confidence looked them up and down. A little smirk painted on his face as he said.

"Shall we try this again?"

Mickey standing like an oak, just hoping that either one of the men would cross the boundary line carved on the floor. He actually took pleasure intimidating and roughing up those who'd get pleasure from doing that very same thing to others. You see Mickey wasn't just a huge tough dumb clown.

He was the son of one of the bravest policemen ever to walk a beat in the town of Greenbush Minnesota. Unfortunately for Mickey, his father Bradley was killed; shot to death by street punks that were beating the shit out of a woman on Parks Lake Avenue. Mickey's dad drove up and confronted the little bastards and was subsequently shot to death by them; they also killed the woman just for kicks. I have absolutely no doubt in my mind, that's the reason Mickey does what he does. He holds a certain degree of honor in helping those incapable of helping themselves. Not smart enough to pass a state entry level test to join the police force…….but brave, tough, and dependable…..yes.

"Shall we try this again?"

"Look!" The little blond haired man said. "We don't want any trouble here!"

"It's too late for that pal!" Mickey barked. "Now who are you? And what are you doing here?"

Mickey took two steps forward, his large shoulders just barely fitting thru the entrance to Ann's kitchen. The two men glanced at each other and made a bee line for the door. Mickey averted their escape attempt by placing himself, that huge massive bulk of a road block, directly into their path. With no way out, they hastily searched around the room. Trapped, caught, and pinned down. With only one other route to avail themselves with they took it. Smack thru the front picture window. Having to stand there in complete and total disbelief, Jason could only look over at the big one and laugh.

"Can you believe that shit?" Jason asked in amusement.

"Oh, I'm sorry boss, I didn't even think of covering the window," he replied remorsefully.

"Hey Mickey, don't sweat it, I'm glad to see them go. I'm not used to this kind of thing. The whole episode made me very uncomfortable."

Staring around the room and taking note of all the broken glass that covered Ann's living room. Jason took it upon himself; making it his responsibility to restore her house to the once simple but comfortable dwelling she enjoyed. After calling a renovator to come as quick as humanly possible, he suggested Mickey accompany him back to his house to check on the girls. While the drive was short and brief, Jason took the opportunity to offer Mickey a permanent position as a bodyguard. Mickey was thrilled to accept the offer. He knew as did everyone else in town, the kind of money Jason had. He was beyond rich and quite possibly one of the most powerful men in the state. Jason left him with just one standing order; make sure nothing happened to Ann. He told him to stick to her like glue. They routinely gave Mickey five hundred dollars for a night of his services, so Jason asked him if two thousand a week was worth his while. A misty eyed Mickey looked down as to not show the glee he was feeling after such a generous offer. No one ever took him as more than a one night bruiser, to give him the respect and the responsibility for someone else's day to day protection was the opportunity he longed for. At last; he could attain some degree of respectability for himself in the eyes of the community.

Cindy and Ann came rushing out the house when they seen Jason's car pull in. A note of anticipation and distress was unilaterally depicted on both girls' faces. When Cindy got a glimpse of Mickey she immediately got even more concerned.

"Relax honey, its ok now. Mickey was there to take care of everything."

"To take care of what Jason, who were they?"

"I don't know Cin; they took off before I had a chance to find out."

A surprised yet relived Ann soon took center stage in the questioning department.

"So you didn't find out what they wanted Jason?" She asked.

"No, not exactly Ann; I think you'll have to stay here for a little bit. Mickey is now going to stay here as well to make sure nothing happens ok."

"That's sure is good to know Jason," Ann commented.

"Do you mean here, here?" Cindy asked nervously.

"Yes!" he snapped. "I mean here!"

Cindy knew well enough to leave well enough alone. Jason had never been the type to go back on a decision once his mind was made up, besides if he thought it was necessary to hire Mickey full time…….. Yes it must have been a hairy ordeal he had encountered and surely they would need his presence around the house. Not a hundred percent sure how to proceed, Jason went into the house to call the authorities. Cindy and Ann followed close behind and behind them …….Mickey.

Chapter 19

"Yes Mr. President I understand, but what you're failing to grasp Sir; is there was absolutely no way we could prepare for this type of scenario!"

"Yes Sir we already did."

"No Sir we won't sir."

"Yes sir, I'll see to it myself Sir."

"Yes Sir thank you Sir."

Hanging up the phone, it was clear and extremely evident the general just got his ass handed to him by the one and only power on the planet that could do so. If tensions weren't high enough this was certainly going to put it thru the roof. General Cobbs took a minute to collect his thoughts. His face turn beat red, as the reaming out; he just suffered by way of the President lingered in his mind.

"Now hear this each and every one of you: It is our job to ensure the safety and security of our illustrious nation. As you all are well aware, for some unknown reason we have lost ships, air craft, and hundreds of men in this exact area. This will go on no longer. If that means staying out here till the end of time I promise you; that will be our course. Under no circumstance are you even so much as permitted to think of leaving here before this bull shit is solved. I want all ships concentrating their efforts on the data we were able to ascertain before the melt down of our so called high-tech computers. I hold everyone in this room personally responsible. Do not, on any circumstance let me down again…..Dismissed!"

The reaction and subsequent thrashing general Cobbs just handed down was not only fitting but necessary. The men had to realize the magnitude of the events that faced them. Their training could make up for the lack of Intel and all the people serving in the fleet were highly trained and well versed at

Mortal combat, however the general knew he must remain stern and seem in total control if he was to get them thru this unknown threat. That was his job.

The rest of the crew dispensed however, Captain St. Jean remained seated. When the last officer had left, the captain stood up, walked to the door and closed it. Turning to the general he said.

"Don't you think that was just a little bit harsh Uncle Ken?"

"Look Patrick, there's something going on here that we have absolutely no clue how to handle. If the crew for one minute assumes we've lost the ability or even the upper hand in any situation were done for. It's taken a hundred years of training, scheduling, strategically placing troops in friendly countries. I can't even imagine the countless amounts of money we've invested into the military and to the image we try so inexorably to display. The entire world must see us as we portray ourselves, powerful, diligent, and most of all unattainable. For all the wars we fought, or help create, nothing says more of our resolve than to explain the unexplainable. This isn't just a freak oddity; it's a chance once again to prove to the world that we are indeed the utmost power on earth. And with that intent, our significance and dominance must start here."

"I understand that uncle I really do. I think I would have approached things differently is all."

The general allowed a little smirk to emerge from his otherwise stringent chiseled face. Maybe to reassure his nephew he should think positively; even in the presence of strife.

"I'll tell you what 'Colonel' when you're a general, you can command in any way you see fit. Until then scrutinize and ascertain but never judge."

He knew full well his uncle was right of course, I assume he wanted to impress the thought that he had a measure of command and a way of manipulating his desires in a form that wouldn't be as abrasive, and yet still achieve the directives from the president. If the general was all he was cracked up to be; he'd take his nephew's point of view and implement it; with his own interweave of course.

Back at the Shield ….

I needed to talk with Mason alone. I had to find out what it was Jennifer had explained to him. I didn't want it to seem too obvious, so I asked him to show me his hut. While walking over I whispered to him low enough not to be heard by anyone,

"Mason I think we might be in vast trouble here!"

"Aw come on Uncle Mike, what does that mean?"

"I don't want to alarm you, but Carl just told me we can't leave here, even if we wanted."

"Ya, I know; we have to sit at the bottom of the ocean for a spell. It has some thing to do with navel ships and stuff on the surface; what about it Uncle Mike?"

"That doesn't concern you at all?"

"No, should it?"

"I should think so Mason. It concerns the hell out of me."

"Uncle Mike, I'm sure you're just overreacting to the differences between this place and what we think of as normal. Besides I love it here, people are friendly, kind; they just seem to want to help each other and us. Is that so bad?"

I had a hard time trying to make heads or tails of this whole mess, and here Mason was talking as if he's lived here his entire life. What could Jennifer have told him to make him so understanding. Is it possible the resonator had some kind of effect on his mental capacity? Did it make him mature over night?

By the time we reached his hut, Mason was already giving me the cold shoulder. It was very apparent when he said.

"Well here it is, knock yourself out!"

"What's come over you Mason?" I asked sarcastically.

"Me, what's with you? First you bring me to this fantastic and almost magical place, and then you tell me it might have been a big mistake. Well from where I'm standing it looks like you're the only one not happy here. Jennifer was right!"

"Right? About what?"

"Maybe you're too old to appreciate it here."

Now my concerns turned to fluster. What was he saying? I'm Uncle Mike. His buddy: the one guy who never judged him or expected anything from him. All the time we spent together, the close bond I thought we shared seemed to have dissipated thru the night. What the heck was happening here.

Before things escalated any further, I decided to return back to my hut. Maybe I wasn't hearing things correctly or just shaken up over the drop in pressure. I couldn't think of a response so I thought it better to just give him some space.

Walking back I was met by Jennifer who just happened to be the one person I was hoping to run into. Obviously I wanted to confront her as to the conversation she had with Mason. As I approached her, I could already tell this was going to be less then cordial. Her stagger towards me was a dead give away. I started to get the feeling everyone was against me. How did something so good turn so bad?

"Could I have a minute please Jennifer?"

"All right, Mike. What would you like?"

"Mason was telling me this morning that you were talking to him last night. I was just curious what you've been telling him."

"Nothing that would concern you Mike, basically we talked about how things run around here, and why."

"I see; it's funny that prior to last night Mason and I had a bond not easily broken but today however it seems as though he couldn't be bothered to give me the time of day. Don't you think that's a bit weird?"

"Not especially Mike, considering in his whole life he's been catered to like a spoiled brat. There's a price to be paid for all that material giving. It makes another wise well balanced kid turn into a self-centered, ego maniac. I do believe the technical term is geocentric."

"What Mason! He's the most down to earth kid you'll ever meet. How can you say that without even knowing him?"

"What makes you think I don't know him Mike?"

"I have a hard time to believe that in a hand full of days you could ascertain and deduce such a detailed characteristic diagnosis."

"That's because you really don't comprehend the parameters surrounding the Shield. Its like this Mike, Every one of us has a distinct characteristic that is harnessed, enhanced, and virtually exploited to its fullest form here. You might think of it as a gift. Something or some talent that is naturally present and innate in us; in every person to be frank. But here, the boundaries of uncertainty and ridicule are dispersed. We become the outlet our persons were naturally supposed to be, enhanced to the utmost maximum of human capability."

"Is that what you call it? I think it more likely to be called brain washing myself. Sounds to me as if you take an interest one has in a certain field and exploit it to make someone think they're destined to do that and only that!"

"Once again Mike you're not getting it. But I don't blame you. It's your narcissistic image emerging from your very core that makes you doubtful and skeptical of our intent here."

"That's comforting to hear Jennifer. So tell me, why was I brought here to begin with?"

"We thought you were a sure fit based on the fact of your mother dying at giving you birth, your father a recluse, and yet you still found the gusto to create the program that catapulted you to fame and fortune. We thought you held an attitude and strength that could be harnessed into a type of harmonist bliss: that would benefit all of us. We were simply mistaken."

"What, the perfect clan, the ultimate humans, wrong? Is that even remotely possible? That's kind of hard to take wouldn't you say. I mean after all, you know all, you see all!"

"Now you're just being contrary Mike and I don't like it! Good bye!"

As she walked away I knew without a doubt this was the biggest mistake I have ever made. What's more, I brought Mason into the grip of hell. Its bad enough to have let myself get ensnared into the heart of evil, but there's no excuse for involving Mason........{IGNORANCE IS BLISS}.

Shutting the door to my hut, I sat on the soft pillowed mattress and tried to put some kind of perspective on the events that just transpired. Anyway I looked at it I was screwed!

Back on the surface......

Three days had past since the out burst of general Cobbs. The men were motivated to say the least and they all worked their asses off to ensure their posts and terminals were manned at all times. Everything was done by the book, protocol was held to the letter. There was a dedication to detail and by no unspoken terms a means to it. The convoy was running like a fine oiled machine; just as general Cobbs ordered. By the night of the third day they had a plan in the works to take a deep sea expedition to the very bottom of the ocean. There was no way it could be a manned excursion, as the depth would be crippling to anyone who'd make the attempt. Instead they opted for a remote controlled sub-erasable. From the surface they could easily confirm whether or not there was something down there in relative safety.

"Sir, we are ready to go with operation sneak peek."

"Very well, commence with departure procedures. People, lets get this right the first time," General Cobbs, suggested.

The anticipation was high and the expectation even greater. Finally after all these years, the answer to the Bermuda Triangle was close at hand; hopefully. Not the most extravagant looking object, with all its devices sticking out everywhere, but the sea hog, as it was known by, was state of the art machinery. Even though it was only six feet long and just about as wide, it was capable of the kinds of things only dreamt of in years past. For one the hog could fly to a depth of ten thousand feet and still maintain its hull integrity. The double thick titanium skin was strong enough to hold a panel of four inch thick Morizite (A translucent material resembling Plexiglas only much stronger) It allowed the sea hog to take photographs in extremely deep water. It also has a portal window made of the same material in order to allow the surface to navigate thru any condition; A true scientific marvel.

"Releasing main cable bindings," the freshly graduated cadet announced.

"Prepare to bring about casting pad for torpedo launch," he continued.

With all eyes fixed on the youngest member of the crew he spelled out the countdown……three, two, and one……

"Sea hog, up and running sir. All systems are operating under normal parameters," the guidance officer said. "We are stream lined to the bottom sir. Running at nine knots; forty-five degree down angle," he added.

"Very good, sonar, report all contacts regardless of how minuet they may seem," the general ordered.

It took approximately twenty four minutes to reach the bottom. Hovering at a depth of 6855 meters, the sea hog arrived at its prescribed location.

"My orders were very specific corporal!" Blasted general Cobbs. "You were to report all contacts!"

"I have general, I can't explain this. There has been no contact by anything what's so ever. Not so much as a sardine has swum across the electronic field sir."

"Is that dam thing flitching again?" Cobbs asked.

"No sir, you could see clearly all the ships in the fleet. Barons beneath the surface are holding steady at mark, 644 bearings 318 sir. It's working sir, there's just nothing here; no aquatic life at all sir."

"Can't be, that's impossible," the general replied.

"I have to speak with you general!" Captain St. Jean demanded.

"In a minute Captain," the general answered.

"No sir, I need to speak with you now sir!" he reiterated while opening the steal door that led to the hallway.

"Very well Captain, radar keep your eyes peeled for any movement what so ever!" he ordered as he marched out of the room.

Making sure there was no one in the corridor, Captain St. Jean, speaking softly addressed the generals concern about the equipment.

"I've been monitoring the electro-magnetic pulse that caused all the mayhem. It came from a field harmonic unknown to any of the frequencies' registered in the main frame computers. When I tried to duplicate the harmonic, the computer spit out 'incapable'. Uncle Ken I think we're in way over our heads."

"Look Pat, I've tried to tell you we can't arbitrarily leave without an explanation to this anomaly!"

"I'm not suggesting that we leave, but I do think we could retrieve the evidence we need by modulating the sea hog with a magnetic pulse receiver. If there is something down there; which I'm certain of, a magnetic pulse receiver will conciliate that which the computers can't identify."

The general was impressed not only with his nephew's prowess, but in the way he qualified his thesis. Arguably, he had put a considerable amount of thought into his proposal. With the new found evidence that indeed there was something amidst down at 6855 meters, the general complied with Captain St. Jean suggestion.

With the order from general Cobbs to return the sea hog to the surface it was retrofitted with the magnetic pulse receiver. Once lowered yet again the pulse beacon was initiated. The impact was instantaneous; the field harmonic sensors went off immediately. A localized distortion was emanating from directly below. As the hog swam deeper and deeper the more intense the field grew. When reaching the 6855 meter mark the out put of magnetic resolution that was registering within the sea hog relays was immeasurable. Considering the capability of the vast and extensive properties the aquatic sleuth had at its disposal, it was irrefutable. At last; concrete evidence was obtained. Inexplicable, however implausible, but never the less realized. Excitement swiftly engulfed the crew; a frenzy of fortuitous information rapidly filled the data banks to the relief of all aboard. The tension surrounding the situation was soon eclipsed by the overwhelming gratification of a successful and over due brake thru. While still rout with uncertainty, even the general seemed to denote the slightest glimpse of optimism. The fact that some sort of theory could derive from the information taken from the sea hog was just the ammunition the general needed to further and more intensely motivate his troops. With the rising of the hog the information collected from the direct contact with the oceans surface could easily be studied. Any oddity could then be scrutinized over with some degree of certainty. This entity, this mystery, had taken a path of elucidation……..so they thought.

MEANWHILE DOWN BELOW …..

Dazed and confused I tried to find comfort in my little dwelling. A few hours past, and I found myself longing for the mundane rituals of my pre-Shield life. As sure as I was of being ostracized by everyone at the Shield and unpleasant as that felt I was even more distressed by the reaction of Mason. Lulled into a false sense of security, he may just find himself lost in this extraordinary world of lies and deception. The possibility and probability of getting him out of here was remote. What was I going to tell Jason and Cindy? How could I have let this happen? Wallowing in self pity came natural for me, all of a sudden I was back in the living room watching my father waste away in front of the television, bereft of life……my god I'm him. The striking thought barely had time to register before the door to my hut opened. Looking up in a hapless, weary way; I saw the sight of a redeeming angel. Please I thought to myself, don't let her cast me away into oblivion as well. She didn't say a word at first; she must have talked to Carl or Jennifer. Walking to my side she reached down and sympathetically placed her placid hand on my sunken leaden shoulder. It sent a rush of reprieve coursing thru my very being.

"Mike, we have to talk."

"I know what you are going to say Charlene, I really messed things up!"

"That's not what I was going to say, but you did screw up. What I was going to tell you is that Carl and Jennifer as well as a few others, think you should leave, but I'm not one of them."

"Charlene, I have to tell you, I'm not crazy about being here anymore either. If it wasn't for the help Mason needs to get healthy I'd be leaving as well."

"You'd want to leave me Mike?" she asked harshly.

"Well no, but it doesn't look as if I'll be given the choice," I replied.

"I see what you mean Mike," She said.

I could tell she had something on her mind but she was reluctant to speak. Trying to make it easy for her I said "You know you could tell me anything right?"

She stared sharply into my eyes and whispered.

"There is one thing that I think you ought to know Mike."

"Yes, and that is?"

"When you first came here, we performed a medical scan on you without your knowing. I couldn't tell you what we found because we didn't know if you were ready to stay or not. But now I guess there's no point in not knowing."

"Know what?" I asked completely startled.

She took a deep breath. I could still remember the look on her face. It was the look of death.

"You have a tumor Mike, deep in the cerebral cortex."

"What? A tumor?" I questioned.

"I'm sorry Mike, really I'm very sorry."

"Well what do we do? Doesn't the magnetic thing-a-ma-jig get rid of all this? I mean it's helping Mason right! What about me?"

"The trouble with your tumor Mike is that it isn't caused by an impurity, it's just one of those things that happen, and regrettably there's nothing we can do for it. If you'd stay here, yes eventually the resonator would shrink the tumor to a minuet particle, but as things are now they want you gone. I really don't know what to do."

When she finished speaking she clinched on to me and broke out in tears. I was completely taken back by her announcement, and regretting the last argument I had with Jennifer. Things started to come together. If they knew the whole time I had this tumor, then why was I here? From what I've seen and heard thus far, these people didn't leave anything to chance. I didn't buy it for a minute when Jennifer told me they had made a mistake. Was this a test? Was I being set up? Was Carl trying to see if I was worthy of the cure from the Shield? Man what a fool I was. What a fool. While I was receiving a bit of comfort with Charlene nestled deep in my chest those words kept rolling over and over in my head; a tumor, a tumor. With a sudden and unexpected jolt, Charlene lurched up glancing intently at the band encompassing her tiny wrist.

"Oh my, I've got to go Mike!" She said stammering towards the door.

"What, what's wrong now?"

"I'm not sure yet, but when this thing [pointing at the bracelet] goes off, it's never good. I'll be back as soon as I can Mike."

She scurried over to the main communications hall, awaiting her arrival stood Carl, Jennifer, and Diane. Clearly, bothered and irate.

"This can't be good…..is it?" Charlene inquired.

"No it isn't! Snapped Carl

"I should say not!" added Jennifer.

"What happened?" Charlene asked.

"I think you'd better look at the diagnostic terminal Charlene. I believe we'll have no choice this time. What's worst is we have to use their blasts." Carl said regrettably.

Charlene scrutinized over the view screen in total disbelief, a mortifying image cropped up as she imagined the horror that was about to be implemented on the surface fleet. She wasn't a willing participant in the terror; still, she was obligated to stay the course set out by the collective. After pleading to counsel who had gathered for this important and decisive action, her idea to stay fixed at the bottom of the ocean and not engage in mortal combat was quickly dismissed. The summery judgment of the Shield was dreadfully clear; the fleet circling above encroaching on their territory moves out of the area on their own accord, or the Shield will move them out permanently.

With the last tenure of a peaceful resolution consumed, the inevitable was at hand. A plan was in the works to completely obliterate the threat from up above. The whole assembly recognized the implication of this action however anticipating the alternative found it necessary. {The reality of it all was made all too unambiguously latter}

"Commence the descrambling of the ballistic missiles located on the Presidio! Make certain only two warheads are activated with the spread to detonate twenty meters below surface level," Carl ordered.

Distinguishing she had no other recourse in averting this unfavorable action, Charlene simply slipped away declaring as she departed.

"I hope this doesn't come back to bite us all in the ass!"

Chapter 20

According to the police there wasn't much they could do. An investigation of course was to commence, but the veracity of the situation would probably end up unsolved. It wasn't like the local investigators were going to spend an absorbent amount of time and energy looking for what seemed to be a simple case of break and enter. Jason deemed it was his responsibility to acquire the answers to the intrusion of Ann's house. After all, she was the main squeeze of one of his best friends. Even though Steve was no longer among them, she was still regarded as a close and trusted friend.

Cindy had all ready unpacked their belongings, seeing as there wasn't going to be a weekend get away to Vegas. She started to cook up Jason's favorite meal consisting of Chicken Cordon Bleu with garlic buttered shrimp and scallops. If anything was going to make him feel better, it was going to be that. Ann supervised the whole expedition adding in her own little dash of curry; knowing Jason loved hot and spicy food she thought it would please him as well. It wasn't as though they had much experience with the hiring of a full time body guard; in fact, other than the odd leasing of Mickey's services they never had the need. Strange as it may be for multimillionaires with the power and prestige as that of Jason and Cindy, but the need never came up. For all intensive proposes they really enjoyed a secluded life for people in the lime light. So as it were, Mickey not only ended up having dinner with the three of them, he also happened to be invited to stay on a permanent bases right there in Jason's house. Mickey immediately accepted of course, and after dinner Jason showed him up to the extraordinarily well furnished spare room in which Mickey could now call home. Comical in a way, seeing as Mickey; the former low life of Greenbush Minnesota was now not only associating with the upper echelons of high society, he was living with them; in essence; he had become one in the most unbridled case of fortune ever bestowed on such a character. Unilaterally, Jason changed the bleak or other wise desolate course of Mickey's providence

The next few weeks flew by without incident. Mickey became accustomed to living the high life all too quickly. He remained diligent as ever when it came to the house security. Conversely to his former self, when the opportunity arose to experience the complexities of mingling with the elevated members of society, he took every advantage of it. With the purchase of a few perfectly tailored new suits and matching footwear along with the endless unwavering assistance of Ann, the new and improved Mickey promptly became somewhat of the male version of a debutante. Ann spent countless hours coaching, tutoring him in the art of properly introducing himself, making small talk, and preparing him to recognize when it would be deemed appropriate to break into a conversation. A typical woman wanting to change the once enormous, socially inept lummox into someone refined or otherwise renovated for social dialogue. Mickey himself seemed to enjoy the rigors of the intense lessons Ann had afforded him. He was truly enthralled in developing his own image as that of fitting in. Mickey was a quick study, eager and captivated with his new-fangled circle of acquaintances. He was therefore motivated to the extreme of enhancing his appearance and shedding the 'big moron' title he once held. Thus exhuming himself as a proper well managed sophisticate like those he encountered.

Jason: meanwhile was pleasantly pleased with the difference in Mickey's attitude and he commended him on the progress he made in such a short period of time. Admittedly he told Mickey he never thought he could make such a change. Not that it was impossible for an individual to change his vocation; it's just Mickey of all people Jason thought would be the most unlikely sort to do so. Mickey himself had to laugh when Jason told him what he was thinking. He wasn't offended by Jason's remarks; in actual fact no one was more surprised then himself. It was amazing how the two of them started to really gel together. What started out as a necessary safety stop had blossomed into a genuine friendship!

Each morning Mickey would make the rounds checking the house and the grounds for anything out of the ordinary. He then returned to the house where Jason had a fresh hot cup of coffee waiting. They'd talk for hours on end; Jason was completely fascinated with the life Mickey had lived. They discussed things that most people never even think of as being the slightest bit interesting. I used to think I knew my two buddies very well {Jason& Steve}. Now that Steve's gone; I thought it would drive Jason and me even closer, that wasn't the case. Yes; he was still a very close friend and I would do anything for him alas things never were the same after we hit the big money…. never. I think it's an impossibility to even ruminate the idea that things would have gone on the way they were when we were adolescents. I assume that was just wishful thinking on my part. Seldom does a day go by in which I don't reminisce back to the 'Mance Manure' days and ponder the theory of how life would have turned out if I hadn't invented the software.

The dawning of a new day began with the cascading moon having been overtaken by the balmy surging sun. In a stream like fashion, strings of lilacs danced feverously on either side of the driveway, penetrating a purple glow on the sides of Jason's shiny new Bentley. A swift prevailing breeze carried the sweet bouquet of lilac coursing thought-out the neighborhood. Jason's property consisted of eight hundred feet of frontage, guarded securely by a ten foot high reinforced forged steel linked fence. Mickey still walked past the entire grounds on his daily routine. That morning he stumbled across some footprints that didn't seem to have an origin. It was as if they just appeared. He was certain he hadn't missed them the day before. After a few concentrated moments of deductible reasoning, he expeditiously retreated back to the main house. Running in haste and vexed with the most gruesome possibilities entranced in his mind, he shifted it into high gear. As he neared the front door he braced himself for the impact. Tensing his shoulders he bolted directly thru the entrance. With the shattering sound of the door collapsing from the colossal force exuded by the panicked giant, it took no time at all to waken the entire house. Jason tentatively approached the scene only to discover his hefty employee standing in the middle of the debris that once was his front entrance door.

"What the hell Mickey! What's wrong!" he snapped.

"Where are Cindy and Ann?" Mickey demanded.

"They're sleeping, or at least they were. What's going on here?"

Mickey promptly jutted past Jason, scurrying down the hall to first check on Cindy. He cautiously stopped in front of her bedroom door. Placing his ear close to the door, he strained himself to hear if there was activity inside. He was startled when Cindy unexpectedly flung open the door. Taking a step backward Mickey could only summon the words.

"You ok?"

"Sure, but what's with this entire rumpus this morning Mick?" Cindy inquired.

"I'll explain in minute Cindy. I have to look in on Ann!" he said as he took off in the opposite direction. Moving fast he took the spiral stairs three at a time to the top. Turning to his right he leaped past his own room and across the sitting room that lead him to Ann's room. Even from a fair distance from her room he could hear the unmistaken sound of her walk in closet door rolling open. Not wanting to make another mistake, yet still in the protective mode, Mickey approached her door and knocked while saying. "Is everything all right in there Ann?" With no response from within her room and as a consequence to his earlier finding he felt he had no choice but to barge in. Looking around the copiously perfectly and extraordinarily furnished room, Mickey found no sign of Ann what so ever. The bed looked as if someone had slept in it and the door to her private washroom was opened. Mickey walked over to the balcony and opened the bi-folding doors. Walking out on to the plush burgundy carpeting which covered the entire solarium overlooking the backyard, he took a quick inventory of the surroundings. He noticed no apparent differences from his higher vantage point. Turning back into the bedroom he found himself face to face as it were with a buck naked and astonished Ann. She promptly averted his line of view seizing the pink silk comforter titivating her bed. Unsure as to how he should respond to the delicate situation, Mickey could only mutter "I thought you might need me so I ….."

Ann immediately recognized his embarrassment with the circumstances; however letting him off the hook was not in her sketch. I guess her vexatious demeanor got the better of her or perhaps she just simply wanted to entice Mickey a bit further.

"What do you mean you thought I might need you?" she asked in a completely seductive tone.

"I meant to say I, I, I, had reason to think there might be something wrong."

"Did you now, or is it something else?" she asked with a little smirk.

The blood rushed to Mickey's face with her indulgence of lustful playing. To him, a hot sophisticated alluring woman would normally be totally out of his reach but circumstances as they were made her somewhat attainable. If he was to make some kind of play towards her, and she wasn't receptive, that might just end the new and invigorating life he was now enjoying. No, the cost of such an endeavor was too much to risk. He would wait for a clearer and more direct tactic.

With the immediate danger put aside for the moment, Mickey returned downstairs to deal with his destruction of his boss's front door. Expecting to get blasted for his actions, he crept slowly into the dinning area and sat across from Jason and Cindy. He immediately told them of the new set of footprints he discovered and that he thought there might have been someone in the house. Feeling like an idiot for overreacting, he slumped in his chair and braced himself for the outpour of hostility he was sure he was in for. Jason looked at Cindy then back to Mickey.

"You just keep up the good work big guy." Jason told him.

"Were both very happy you're with us Mickey." Cindy added.

Unable to fully express his immeasurable relief, Mickey reiterated it was only his intent to protect them. Jason as well as Cindy knew he was simply doing what they hired him to do. A passing moment with a communal sigh of understanding and the three of them let out a giggle.

"So Mickey, see anything interesting up in Ann's room?" Cindy asked.

"More than mortal man deserves," he replied.

Another collective giggle was released just as Ann entered the dining room, assuming a rudimentary smile.

"Ya, Ya, Ya. He got the full show I know," She said with the tiniest little wink towards Mickey.

Without missing a beat Mickey returned fire with "Well worth the price of admission too."

A simultaneous laugh broke out while Ann gently and rather provocatively tugged on Mickey's chest hairs as she pranced passed him. Was this a more direct and clearer tactic Mickey thought to himself?

Chapter 21

    I woke up with the horrifying revelation of Charlene's diagnosis still ringing in my head. It's hard to put in perspective all the trivial thoughts that seem to linger in one's mind when faced with your own mortality. I was no longer consumed with the pity I felt for not having such a contented life. The sheer fact of living itself was the only demand I could contemplate.

    I really didn't know it until that particular morning, but I couldn't suppress the obvious; I was a coward. My own strength would never be enough to facilitate the amount of positive energy I was going to require to successfully combat this thing. What's more, I had flouted so many people out of my life that would otherwise be capable or at the very least willing to help me thru this dilemma.

    My father told me all my life 'never burn your bridges behind you'. Boy was he right. I realized a different appreciation for him that morning. I began to understand in the most infinitesimal way what he must have gone thru with the passing of my mother. Until now, I had no comparison. The loss of my buddy Steve was disheartening, but facing my own impending demise brought a new indebtedness to my father I never had. Yes, we didn't have fun together, or play catch. Not once do I recall him lifting me up or turning me around to make me dizzy. That being said, he did get up every morning to make me breakfast. I saw the old, faded man that was left after his monumental loss of my mom…..his wife! Yes his wife; that never clicked in 'til right then.

It made me think what kind of son I had been as well. Did I show any kind of thanks or gratitude for what he was capable of giving? When someone close to you dies, it leaves an impression on your own expectancy. When the one you vowed to love for the rest of your life dies, it robs you of any expectancy. That was my realization that day; my epiphany if you will. Poor dad I thought, I wished I could be with him right then to give him a true and understanding embrace. One full of love, appreciation, and regret, for all the negative thoughts I had of him throughout the years. Suddenly the situation I was facing didn't appear as grave.

The knocking on my hut sent me hurdling out of my subliminal pattern and snapped me back into the realm of contemporary realization. In the beaming brightness of light, I made out the sleek silhouette of Charlene. An instant genre of liberation emerged from the former austere state I was in.

By the look on her face the news she had received from Carl was not only alarming but distressful. The flicker of creamy jade now lay dormant in her once emerald green eyes. In its place was the on slot of complete and annihilated failure. It didn't take a genius to see that one. I knew she would get to the discussion she had with the others soon enough, so for the moment I remained as supportive and attentive as possible. That was the one thing I really enjoyed about her; there wasn't any pretentiousness pomposity about her. She told it like it was and if you didn't like the obvious, too bad. She sat with me for about fifteen minutes before she said a single word. As it turned out, the words she did say just about gave me a cardiac. She began….

"The time for uncertainty has come and past Mike. The inevitable is now at hand. Adversely and without my approval, the committee decided to end the standoff with brutal and mitigating force. I'm very disturbed and equally disappointed with the decision."

"What kind of force are you talking about Charlene; you're not speaking of the nuclear kind are you?"

Shrugging her head downward as to escape the question, her silence spoke volumes. I sat there in complete disbelief. What kind of people could do such a thing? What are they a bunch of lunatics?

"I need to speak with Carl right now Charlene! I mean right now!"

"It's not that easy Mike. Right now he's preparing for a major engagement. The worst we have ever encountered to date. There's no way you could get within a hundred meters of him. Besides, you're not the most favorable person around here anymore. I suppose it will all be over in a matter of hours."

Unable to think clearly, I decided to go for a walk and find Mason. Charlene was close behind me as we left the hut. It was unimaginable, the chaos abound and was ever more frantic then earlier when we descended to the bottom. We scurried over to mason's hut only to find it empty. Asking Charlene if she had any inclination as to his whereabouts, she had none.

Drifting aimlessly was proving out to be a waste of valuable time. I was certain Mason hadn't been told of the situation and it was my responsibility to make sure he was safe; even if that wasn't what he wanted or needed.

While the other members of the elite race scampered around the compound, Charlene and I methodically and systematically checked on possible areas Mason may well have trekked. With the amount of energy he possessed along with the sheer amount of exhibits at his disposal, finding him promptly would turn out to be a challenge. We adventured far past the perimeters set out to him by Jennifer and Carl. It wasn't until we came near the very end of the Shield's outer hull that we finally found him. He was basking in the warmth of artificial sky, absorbing the echo of the resonator as it charged up. Not wanting to sound authoritative, I solely asked how he was doing.

"Hey Mason, how are things in this neck of the woods?" I asked jokingly. "What do you care Mike!" he blurted.

That was it! I'd had enough of that crap! Stepping up face to face with him I said angrily "Mason what's going on with you? For the past few days you've been rude, short tempered and now it's like you have no respect for me at all. What have I done so wrong to make you treat me this way? What!"

"I don't know what you're talking about Mike," he said.

"How about that Mason now its Mike: not Uncle Mike, just plain Mike. You don't find that a bit strange Mason?"

"Not really, it's not as if your actually my uncle now is it?"

His demeanor had changed into something completely foreign. This wasn't the boy I brought here. He wasn't the boy I watched grow up. This wasn't the boy who'd stolen the hearts of all the ladies working at May-moo Tech. And this certainly wasn't the young man who was going to run my company; not anymore.

Walking away from the insolent little bastard made me sick. At that point I had no ambition what's so ever about anything. I didn't care about a damn thing. Life was going down hill in a hand cart. Rushing to catch up, Charlene called out for me to slow down, but slowing down wasn't going to happen. I wanted out! .... O.U.T............

Trotting beside me she reached out for my arm, grabbed it and pulled me towards her. I noted a glimpse of pride in her eyes. This was most confusing as she knew what Mason meant to me. And yet even as she witnessed the attitude he developed, it didn't have any affect on her. The hurt in my face must have been self-explanatory because she let go of my arm and tenderly wrapped her arms around my waist saying

"I know how hard this must be on you and I understand Mike, truly I do. What you have to remember is the attitude that he is portraying is simply his natural ability coinciding with his genetic make up of leadership pushing thru. He is going thru so many metaphysical changes; I doubt very much he is even aware of the things that are happening right now. He loves you, respects you, and needs you; even if he doesn't 'need you' understand?"

"No I don't understand," I whispered. "If he loves me, why is he treating me like I'm a 'nobody'?"

"He isn't Mike. He just has to be all that he was meant to be. His hormones are running so fast and furious, not to mention the adrenalin coursing thru him at a record pace. It's no wonder he's standoffish. For the first time in his young life he realizes his place. Mike, Mason is a natural born leader. Every part of his being at this time is telling him to take charge and assume command. The only trouble is he has no life experience that could allow him to understand what that genuinely means. He is processing information that would normally be unattainable, and then suddenly poof there it is. It's not his fault."

The sobering explanation as to Mason's new identity left me somewhat bewildered. It wasn't like I understood his dilemma or the transformation he was living. Even with Charlene's assurance that he was only carrying out his genetically engineered properties, I couldn't help feeling betrayed. Disconcerting as it was to accept, I had to. The idea that my little buddy had such gargantuan potential was the only mechanism that could perpetuate a continued hope towards things turning out favorably.

The situation between the surface fleet and the Shield was intensifying to its horrific pinnacle. With superior technology at their disposal combined with the unmitigated willingness to vanquish the theoretical threat, an outcome of victory was not only expected but unequivocally assured. While the anticipation of incursion was placed midst stage, the general assembly for midday dining assumed its normal course.

"How could they possibly think of food at a time like this?" I asked dumbfounded.

"Each and every person here has complete confidence in the structure of command. They know as well as I, there's nothing that could possibly interrupt life here. That's why to them it's like nothing is happening at all. Sure they'll get a rush of emotion with the hustle of preparation for the encounter, but the reality is that nothing is ever left to chance. This conflict was over before it got started."

"That sounds like you have a trace of boastfulness in your theory Charlene," I said.

"No, not boasting when it's a fact Mike. Our family didn't start or put in motion what is about to happen. They did. I think if you step back and look at this from a more philosophical point of view, you'll reach the same conclusion as we did. The serenity of the Shield will and must be maintained at all cost. We believe that one day, mankind will possess the intelligentsia it will take to understand and appreciate the harmony that we strive for. The acrimony that they still portray to each other tells us that for now, your kind is still ages away from not only understanding the Shield, but the vast majority would not even accept the Shield or its principles," she explained.

"You may be right about the way things go on in the normal world. There are evil sons-of-bitches everywhere. Yes, society as a whole is lied to and dictated as to what to love and hate. Sure we don't know half the things that go on and if we did it would most likely make our heads spin. Does that give you the right to harbor hostility towards those who don't have the advantages you possess?"

"We don't hold any hostility towards anybody here Mike."

"Sure you do, you just do it from another vantage point. If you really had that much concern for your fellow man, you'd make every effort to rid the sufferings of those less fortunate! If you allow injustice to stifle those who can't protect themselves, that makes you just as guilty as the oppressors themselves. Anyway you slice it, it's immoral."

"Sorry you feel that way Mike. If you had seen the things I have seen, you might see this occurrence as more than it appears."

I knew immediately I hurt her feelings. If the situations were reversed I'm sure I would be feeling the same way, but they weren't. Endeavoring to maintain civility had become more difficult second by second. With the impending destruction of the surface fleet, and with no option availed to me, I modestly returned to my quarters. Charlene stayed behind with a look of discontent painted on her melancholy face. Perhaps I just lost the only advocate I had remaining in my corner in this putrid, rancid place.

"Carl, the interface connections have been collated and the reprogramming of silos five and six have been implemented. I'm waiting for the startup confirmation," Jennifer explained.

"Very good, commence operation in fifteen minutes. Make certain all pressure locks had been calibrated to absorb deflection impact and close off air ventilation system. Bring the resonator pulse back online and prepare to engage deterioration field. What is the approximate detonation time once we start initiation sequencing?" Carl asked.

"It will take the magnetic band two seconds to reach the system on the Presidio. The interface will initiate immediately causing their security system to override safety protocol. From that point it will take sixty-five seconds to start launch program. Assuming the breakdown in communications will likely cause a few seconds of confusion, in all probability there would be no delay in launch confirmation. From that point we have fifteen seconds to abort if you wish to do so," Davis added.

With a momentary pause and a swift dissertation of the situation, Carl gave the word……………

"Initiate!"

Chapter 22

ABOARD THE PRESIDIO ……

Each of the crews worked frantically on all shifts trying to decipher the information collected from the sea hog, the captain reported all progress to General Cobbs. General Cobbs in turn was in constant contact with the pentagon, which was in direct contact with the President. Having the situation in hand and a resolution to this enigma within reach, General Cobbs assured the pentagon that he would have an explanation to ratify the discombobulating of their computer system. He also expressed the need for additional time to further accentuate clarity in this matter. Once given the green light with absolute dominion in this matter, the general estimated and reported the solution was imminent. His confidence was unparalleled and beyond illusion…….. [HIND SIGHT IS 20/20].

"Sir, we just lost diagnostic control!"

"Sir, we just lost heading frequencies!"

"Sir we're going into total systems failure!"

Towards a radical turn to the surreal, the General and crew we're spontaneously positioned into a state of anarchy. Dissolution set in immediately following the unimaginable announcement of the ballistic missiles arming themselves in silos five and six. The countdown to deployment had commenced without warning. A nervous energy instantly griped part of the bridge crew, while some of the other officers stood frozen, petrified by the prospect of the consequences about to unfold.

"Sir, missile launch in thirty seconds and counting!" cried the bewildered young helmsman.

"Override the artillery banks and set a new security code!" General Cobbs ordered.

"We can't sir! The computer has locked out all command codes and has initiated launch confirmation; detonation scheduled within one thousand meters of deployment, twenty seconds now sir!" he responded hysterically.

"We're done for!" cried out Sergeant Denis Cooper.

While the horns sounded and the whistles blew and with no other option as time beat down with a suffocating gnash, General Cobbs played his only card left available to him. His only alternative was to send out a distress call and hope someone, somewhere would receive it. He knew full well a blast at that range would obliterate every ship in the fleet, with no chance of survival.

It's hard to imagine what must have consumed his thoughts at that precise moment. Maybe a lifetime of mistakes came rushing to mind; possibly a lost love from his youth past by with a spirit of rekindling desire. Or perhaps the horror of the ultimate judgment obscured his final pulse.

"Ten seconds sir, nine, eight, Seven, six, and five……..

BACK AT THE SHIELD …..

"Abort….abort!" Carl repeated.
"Resolution pulse deactivated," Davis reported.
"Has the system override come back online aboard the Presidio?"
"Yes they have, with two seconds to spare," Jennifer said.

"Well then, let's just see if that worked or not, I'd hate to think of the alternative," Carl commented.

ON THE SURFACE ......

"What the fuck just happened here helm?" the General screamed.
"I'm uncertain sir, I don't know. I don't fucking know!" whimpered the young helmsman trying desperately to hide the gigantic tears that had swelled up in his eyes.
"Ok listen up everyone! I want a detailed explanation as to what the hell just happened. Confirm audio and digital communications with the entire fleet. Let's work this problem people. Don't let fear sway your decisions."
Escaping into the corridor to catch his breath, general Cobbs converged with his nephew Captain St. Jean. The salutes and the yes sir no sirs had been thrown out the window on contact.
"What the hell is going on? One second I'm sleeping in my rack, and then the next I'm hearing the fucking nuclear missile launch sirens going off! What the fuck happened?"
"Relax Pat relax. We had some kind of malfunction with the safety protocol system. It's back on-line and we're working the problems out as we speak."
"Working out the problems, Uncle Ken; the god dam missiles armed themselves. What's there to work out? Let's mobilize the fleet and get the fuck out of here!"
"Now look Pat, I'm putting in a call directly to the president, and he will decide the proper course we should take. I have no call in this now. You know the drill, once we lost control of the main line for any reason, it's his call."
"Uncle Ken, you know he's just going to order us back, let's get out while the getting's good, I have a bad feeling about all of this."
"Steady Pat, the men need to feel that things are progressing on schedule, especially now in light of this latest incident. We can't afford to lax at this point. Look, I was just as taken back by this event as

anyone else. I mean hell I thought I was going to die just as you and the rest of the crew did. But that doesn't give us the right to run. We're Marines god dam it, we stay the course!"

The impact of the General's last words left a bitter taste in the Captain's mouth. Feeling a bit anemic from the ordeal may have beleaguered his judgment for a split second. The one feature the General was renowned for was his aptitude to motivate the men and women under his command. It worked obviously, as Captain St. Jean reevaluated his assessment and concurred with the General; as any good hard fighting tough as nails balls up Marine would do.

"Sir yes sir," were the only words to come out of the Captain. The pride now gleaming from those broad wide shoulders of his and with the echo of the General's courage still ringing in his ears, he proceeded to the main bridge to assume command. He would make dam straight the orders of general Cobbs.

Returning to his quarters Cobbs knew and was expecting the call which he suspected was going to end his career. He followed protocol to the letter however there was no excuse that would render the loss of control of his nuclear missiles acceptable. Any way he looked at it, he was most assuredly in for the most brutal ass reaming in the history of the United States armed forces. He put on a brave face in front of the men no doubt but once attaining the safety and seclusion of his private quarters, his emotions got the better of him. Plunging lifelessly into his black leather worn-out easy chair, he placed his nerve shaken hands to his face. What happened he thought to himself? How was he going to explain this after assuring the pentagon things were in control? What would the other brass think of his command skills? A lifetime of extraordinary service wiped out by one single moment, encapsulated for all time. The pressure and strain he was under was understandably difficult to deal with. That in it self would most likely put to the test any man's resolves. General Kenneth Meric Cobbs, however, was no ordinary man. He nearly single handedly transformed the officers training program at Fort Humbly, into the most modernly advanced progressive academy in the entire world. Every sector and branch of the military sent its best and most elite officers' to attend. The rigorous training was not only that of a militarily focused program moreover he executed and harnessed the intricacies of command strategies as well as that of diplomatic complexity. He knew from his experiences that brut force is only effective if the affected party understands the reasons behind the force. Any nation could very well arm itself and cause global conflict. The real test in that situation as taught by the academy is to understand and deal with the issue that caused the arming in the first place. General Cobbs was instrumental in inciting that very aspect of training into the program. To put it mildly, a group of well trained, fearless warriors are a good thing. While a group of well trained fearless thinkers are unbeatable.

The call General Cobbs was waiting for and expecting came thru as predicted. On the other side of the line was a vastly agitated and perturbed chief of staff Cory Brasher.

"Ok General Cobbs lets have it. The entire White House assembly is waiting anxiously for the reason our nation was put on the highest alert. We really want to know how the commander and chief of the most powerful nation on the planet, is going to explain how his best and most decorated General could allow the infiltration of his nuclear arsenal! What say you General Cobbs?"

"To tell the truth Mr. Brasher, we're still collecting that information as we speak. I can say with a definite point of certainty, the entire crew and fleet for that matter is anxious and on edge. I realize the predicament this situation has placed on the Presidency and for that I am truly regretful. The plain fact is we are no further ahead in explaining this oddity, then any other time in the past. As a point in fact we may be even further behind."

"That's not the riposte we we're hoping to hear General!"

"Unfortunately, Mr. Brasher that's the only answer I can offer at this time. Are Generals Derek Kielipper and Glenn Filston present?"

"Yes we are Ken, and we're equally as puzzled as the rest of the nation. When your silos were invaded, it triggered a nation wide alert system that was secretly implemented by the C.I.A. It seems as the right hand wasn't clear on what the left hand had authorized," General Filston noted.

"Damn it Phil, that means the whole bloody world knows what's happened here!"

"That about sums it up Ken, the question remains what to do about the fallout?" General Kielipper sputtered.

"The consensus here is to back off the fleet and return to dry dock. We'll then go over the data which you have obtained thus far and make our recommendations to the international community. The President is preparing to address the nation as we speak. We all believe this is the only avenue to completely put to ease the understandably heightened concern of the American people as well as that of our allies. For your part you are not to disclose this meeting with anyone, not even the senior staff. Have code 'delta 3' protocol in place by nine-thirty hours, maintain radio communications with the fleet and return to the cape. Is that clearly understood General Cobbs?" ordered the Chief Of Staff Mr.Cory Brasher.

"Perfectly clear Mr. Brasher, perfectly clear. I'll see you soon enough Glenn, Derek," the General remarked as he hung up the phone.

Cobbs took a second to collect his thoughts, and then proceeded to the helm to address the crew. He gave the order to lift anchor and ensue a course returning the desperately nervous fleet to the mainland. With the announcement of the President's national address forth coming, Cobbs allowed the crew the time to avert their attention momentarily to hear their commander and chief's pictorial of events.

LADIES AND GENTLEMEN, MEMBERS OF THE PRESS THE PRESIDENT OF THE UNITED STATES OF AMERICA…………..

"My fellow Americans, I speak to you this day, not only as your President, but as a husband and a father. As some of you in the press are aware, there was an incident in the Atlantic this morning. A rather hazardous, dangerous situation was averted today while on a routine mission of international aid when one of our convoys experienced a total electronic system failure. The majority of you have heard the tales and the stories of the phenomena known as the Bermuda Triangle. Well today the United States Navy found out first hand about the dangers affiliated with this area. Our engineers alongside with a number of top notch environmentalists have been working for years as to better understand the very nature and complexities of this enigma! It wasn't until today we finally have confirmation as to the depth and wide range of its capabilities. I'm no scientist, but I will try to explain what has been explained to me. The triangle is an area in the Atlantic between the points of Florida, Puerto Rico, and Bermuda. Some one million square miles of water! To date, very little was known about the magnetic fields that seem to spring up periodically throughout this vast area of the Atlantic. As Americans, we have long been fascinated and at times even frightened by the stories affiliated with the Bermuda Triangle. For the most part, these stories have been long tales and even down right lies. Exaggerations of long shore seamen desperately trying to portray themselves as brave with the encounters of the great unknown, you get my point. Today mind you the tale of danger was by no means a creation of fiction. At 08:34 this morning, while on route to supply the service men and women who defend this great nation, the destroyer Presidio and her crew stumbled across an electrode magnetic field so strong, with such a direct field harmonic that it scrambled the computers safety override system. This scrambling of the safety system automatically sends out a distress signal though a satellite wave beacon resulting in the emergency broadcast system to initiate. Every radio, television throughout the country was automatically redirected to play the same warning. Return to your homes and stay tuned for further instructions. This system of information was put in place to combat the terrorism threat that continues to plague the world. But I want to assure you, the American public and that of our allies, at no time was the situation out of control. This administration was bombarded with a steady stream of inquiries as to what was happening. Now ladies and gentlemen, the stories picked up by some members of the press were inaccurate to say the least. An investigation is already underway to determine who or by what means these fabrications had been circulated. If there was an impropriety perpetrated by a member of the press causing intestinal fear to streak across this great nation of ours, there will be definite and dire repercussion to that error. The area in mention is a strip of water; known as the Sargasso Sea, just east of the triangle. For safety reasons, it is our contention that all sea bound vessels should and will avoid this area. That is why we are implementing a no fly or passage zone in this area. As of right now, the American Military will impose this restriction. Our friends in NATO and that of our allies assure us of complete and total compliance to this measure. Any incursion into the restricted area will be dealt with in the harshest means possible. Thank you and God bless America."

Customary as it was for the President to answer questions from the press following a public address, he didn't bequeath any sort of Q and A this time. The press room was cleared immediately much to the displeasure of the corp.

Chapter 23

If the acquisition of culture, the social order was attainable to all those who sought to achieve that brand of recognition, the fixation could and would only bring those with that particular sense of snobbery together. The trouble with that opinion consists of the diversity within the social order itself. It would much more benefit those that had culture, as opposed to those who sought culture……. for the two, in my opinion should never mix. Its not that I believe anybody is better than the next person. The plain fact is, if you've grown up with money, style, the opportunity of traveling to exotically remote regions of the globe, like the truly cultured, the understandings of those trapped by the sting of hard work and the daily struggle to survive are inconceivable. The misfortunate may dream of the indulging properties of wealth however they could never escape the reality of a humble beginning. The memories and experiences of that beginning would only pierce thru the veil of pretense. On the other hand, those born into money and culture may strive to understand the oppression sentenced to the unfortunate but could never completely differentiate between craving and need, sympathy and empathy. Accidental or misguided, it equates to a labyrinth of unconscionable deception.

Looking towards one another, Jason and Cindy thought hard about the explanation the President expelled as to the implementation of the emergency broadcast system. They both became exceedingly suspicious by the comments and story unfolding. Jason wondered to himself if there could be a similarity between the happenings on the Presidio and that of the Shield. He distinctively remembered Mike mentioning the overwhelming power source of the Shield and its magnetic frequency. It had to be connected he thought, but he also recounted Mike saying that the Shield was located somewhere near Scotland; that had nothing to do with the troubles in the Atlantic. Or did it?

Walking thru the freshly new repaired front entrance and while taking a second to recall the event for which it was in need of repair, Mickey readily sundered up to Cindy giving her the thumbs up to the security sweep he had just rendered.

"Did you hear the President's address Mickey?" she asked.

"Got the last part of it, boy was he some pissed off with the media," he concluded.

"I'll say, so what do you think Mick, are you and Ann kind of getting a little close or what?" she asked curiously and a bit inquisitively.

"Nah, she's way out of my league," he answered.

"That's not what I heard Mickey boy, that's not what I heard," she said giggling as she scampered past him teasingly.

Intrigued as to how and where she attained that information, he playfully chased her down the corridor of the family room and out the opened patio doors. Laughing as they bobbed and weaved their way thru the backyard, he finally had her cornered between the pool and the diving board. Both trying to catch their breath, while laughing unstoppably, made the event even more amusing.

"So what did you hear and from who?" Mickey asked.

Still having the giggles and unable to respond yet she pointed directly up. Looking upward Mickey noticed Ann watching and enjoying the show from her balcony. He instantly became reserved, thinking it might not look so manly to be frolicking around in the backyard like some school boy however Ann put him to ease when she asked mischievously.

"Can I come out and play too?"

"I think I'll leave that to you guys," Cindy smirked.

Mickey anxiously awaited Ann's decent. He mulled over probable topics he would try to eloquently engross her with without making it obvious he was trying to do so. Walking around methodically planning his best avenue of approaching Ann, he surmised she would probably initiate the small talk as was customary. When she approached him, the scent from her tantalizing sweet perfume was filling his nostrils sending a rush of lustful bliss charging thru his 'appendages'. Her long lustrous blond hair, bounced from side to side enthralling him even deeper. He stood there in front of her completely beguiled, trying desperately in vain to recall his prior thought pattern. He was going to be so cool, so Gary Cooper, he was going to make her fall at his feet. Things turned out just slightly different then expected. Mickey found himself at the opposite end of the spectrum. Unlike the confident, certain, convinced and collected image he was hoping to display, a more befuddled, bewildered, bemused and even baffled Mickey surfaced. He couldn't help it; she was purely the most sensual, splendorous, seductive specimen of female purity he'd ever suffered. This was a woman worthy of his inclusive time, energy and total sincerity. With a woman of her caliber by his side, he needn't feel insecure or timid in any forum he could envision. What's more, by means of an austere glance she could motivate him to the utmost maximum of his potential. Basically, the hefty, generously proportioned Mickey was in love.

"Good morning Ann, sorry if we woke you up," he said as gentlemanly as he could.

"No you didn't, I was up for a while, just didn't feel like getting out of bed," She replied seductively.

"Oh, would you.......like to get some breakfast?" he asked curiously.

"I'm not really hungry Mickey..........not for food anyway," She smutted.

This had definitely been a deliberate advance Mickey concluded. He could endure no more, Enticed to the limit of human acceptance he made his hopefully none fatal move. Slipping to within inches of her, he brushed back her soft silky blond hair with his considerably oversized shaking hand, gently placing it on the side of her blushing flushed check on its return. Gently stroking the side of her left eye with his right thumb, he slowly raised his left hand and cupped it on her right cheek, engulfing it doing so. He could easily feel her tremble and became encouraged by her involuntary movements. Softly and smoothly he raised his head, making certain to glance her chin with his open bottom lip. When his lips confronted hers they locked instantly, inflicting pleasure while yielding an inner thrusting motion from her hips. He may not have been the most sophisticated man on the block but he knew and could recognize her eagerness to advance the program. Still in a tight embrace, Mickey firmly rubbed his strong powerful hands up and down Ann's twitching back, stopping on every down stroke to grasp and hold her gyrating ass cheeks. Her panting only aroused Mickey further. With vivacious dedication they pawed and groped each other to a point that only one conclusion would satisfy their lust. Effortlessly hoisting her up into his immense arms he carried her back to her room, all the while Ann's mouth staying in total contact with his neck. Impressively holding her in one arm, he used the other to close and lock the door. Ann's panting turned to moans of pleasure when he tore her blouse off her body and taking one second in turn to do the same to his. Laying her down on her left side he reached around her and with one sweeping motion discarded the loose set of sweat pants she was wearing. Lying on their sides, Mickey forcibly held behind her while he caressed her body softly rubbing her smooth, sleek thighs from her hips clean down to her ankles. Ann couldn't help but hump her hips forward with each passing turn. Slipping his hand to the front of her midsection and sliding it slowly downward until he reached the top of her silky pink panties, Ann exploded in a wave of delight. Taking a hold of Mickey's hand she opened her long athletic legs and guided him under her wet garment to area responsible for the dampness. Mickey's eyes peeked with amazement when he realized how excited she was. Her scent filled the room as her wetness left nothing hanging but the obvious to Mickey. Still holding his huge hand under her panties and rubbing herself along with him, she desperately plunged their fingers deep into her wet pulsating awaiting gash. Ann instantly burst aloud with a deep and overwhelming howl. She frantically started to groove her trashing hips in synchronized time to the motion of their hands. She could feel the enormous pressure of Mickey's manhood pressing her from behind. Taking her hand out of her own panties allowing Mickey to continue on his own, she tilted her body in order to grab for Mickey's package. Once she unzipped him exposing his open fly she greedily pulled out his member and began massaging him. Within ten seconds they had their timing down delivering unbelievable amounts of tantalizing ecstasy to each other.

"I want you Mickey I want you now!" she screamed.

"You got me baby, boy do you got me!" he exclaimed.

Placing his freakishly large body over hers, he smiled with the delight of this gorgeous sexy woman gazing up at him in anticipation. Wrapping her legs firmly around his waist he entered her as they both let out a cry of passion.

Chapter 24

The hustle outside my hut was all but over; I could hardly sustain my anger. Their unwavering decision to eradicate innocent people left me not only puzzled but worried what the world could expect from this power crazed dilapidated society. I'd show them a thing or two but I lacked the gumption.

With all hope lost, the inevitable depression lurked its ugly face in my direction once again. Confronting the lonely perils of loss by myself, was even more disheartening leaving me in utter dejected misery! What I wouldn't give to go home to avail myself with the comfort of my own bed. If I ever got out of this I told myself, I would never venture any further away than my backyard. I'd take the boring, mundane days and welcome them with open arms. Take my house take my money take my freedom but please leave me my sanity. I guess the leaves don't fall too far from the tree after all.

With the primary reason for my unwarranted expedition to the Shield expelled; that of an adventure, the ever consuming knowledge of having a hand however remote in past events permeated my every thought. I realized I didn't push the button so to speak but either way I was involved. A colossal collection of corrupted calamity, that's what we were. Needless to say I was shocked when Charlene, Carl and Jennifer walked into my hut. The relax euphoria they shared left the single dismal strand of hope that remained to appallingly evaporate. Disgusted and nauseous over their collective unscrupulous skirmish, I was in no mood to discus their self-reasoning.

"Why are you here again? Just let me be, you win you win!" I exclaimed

"You're right of course Mike, as point in fact we did win. Not the way you assume we did however," Charlene indicated.

What was that? A glimmer, a hope, a prospect of chance; is it possible?

"Well then, how your victory is different then I expected?" I asked vividly.

Jennifer and Carl shared a glance then Carl turned to Charlene giving her a tap on the shoulder and said. "You tell him, I think he'll appreciate it from you better."

"You may be right," she agreed.

Giving me a friendly nod, as if to say 'see you later bud' Carl and Jennifer made a hasty exit. The weight of the world felt like it was thrown off me by her beautiful white smile. She moved closer to me and with each step my heart jumped a beat. I was instantaneously engrossed with not only her presence but also the good news I figured she was bringing. What started off as the worst day of my entire existence was going to turn out just fine I believed.

"You didn't do it did you?" I asked

"Yes we did Mike, we set their missiles to deploy and at the last possible second ended the scare off," She explained.

"The scare off?" I repeated.

"That's right Mike, the scare off. Do you really believe we could perpetrate such destruction and anarchy? That's not what we're about Mike, not in the least."

Comforted by her confession of the ploy set out by the Shield, I sank back down on the bed thankful and alleviated that the treachery they considered was merely a bluff. It started me thinking nonetheless, if they did crave to wreak havoc and devastation, nothing on the plant could stop them....nothing.

"I can't tell you how happy and relieved I am that I was wrong Charlene. The circumstances surrounding my outbreak of emotions could be misunderstood as hostile; I think you know it was more nerves than that right?" I asked.

"I know Mike, so does Carl too. That doesn't however excuse the outburst of hostility you expressed towards Mason now does it? I hope you make amends with him because he really thinks you've abandoned him."

"That wasn't my intent Charlene, I felt bad enough just thinking of losing his respect. I might have been angry and hurt by his words because I didn't understand or want to understand this metamorphosis he's undergoing but I would never intentionally hurt him, never."

Smiling at me confirming she acknowledged my atonement and acceptance of Mason's inevitable preordained future potential, a deeper sensation of ease materialized. The laps in mood over the last few days disappeared into oblivion, leaving only the silent bliss of a new and better understanding between Charlene and me. If she held on to a lingering displeasure it wasn't apparent. Not wanting to reopen the wound yet still curious about the affect their stance had been on the military, I probed her a little further for some supplementary information. She was reluctant at first and then came to explain the address the President announced to the nation. Recalling the events as I saw them or understood them to be, what the President said and the true facts had more than a few holes in them to come out to be correct.

Whether or not he lied or was forced to lie to protect the public wasn't my place to judge. It did however unlock my eyes to the possibility that the Shield knew and expected that very response.

"We can resurface by tomorrow morning Mike, there's a no fly zone put in place by your government. That will deter any other spectators from coming within thirty miles of here. Ideally that was our main goal, not to hurt or kill anybody just attain the space we desire to go about our own business." She said.

"So you got what you wanted without one lost soul, isn't that the direction you should have taken?" I asked.

"Yes it was Mike, she said reluctantly. There is something I need to talk to you further about, now seems a good a time as ever," she told me softly.

"And what's that Charlene?" I asked

"Well, it's about you're tumor Mike," She whispered.

With the entire goings on in the last forty-eight hours, I nearly put the dreadful news out of mind but now there it was again.

"So tell me, what's the verdict?"

"I can't say as yet. Mike, we're having a meeting tonight to discus that very thing. I'm not going to lie here; it doesn't look good for you. No not good at all. I'm with you and oddly enough so was Carl but that's only two of the seven people that have a vote. Now we have to expect the best and prepare for the worst. I have!" she concluded.

"How do you mean you prepared for the worst?" I asked perplexedly. "That's not something I could talk about right now Mike, rest assured I won't let you down……I promise."

Her reassuring tone left some hope to remaining at the Shield at least until the tumor had time to fritter away. She was right in one respect; it was a big mistake to jar up the emotions of the others without understanding the process. ………………….. {Hind site is 20/20}.

Carl, Jennifer, Charlene, Denis, Davis and Eric gathered together to argue my fate "Mike Robert James". They each knew the others' stand and the crossfire began.

Jennifer started "So what you're saying Carl, is you believe if given the chance Mike would blend in as a productive part of our family?"

"I'm saying that very thing Jennifer, I think with the right adjustment he could."

Davis broke in "Wasn't it you Carl that first said the chances of him fitting in here were remote at best?"

"I did," Carl replied.

"Then why are you so adamant now that he does belong here, when you yourself thought him a long shot?" Eric questioned.

"Look, I can't say for certain that Mike could change his thought process. I do think however we hold a moral obligation to him. We informed him of his tumor; we can't just drop him off at the corner and wish him well. Jennifer, you're the last word on the medical front, how long would it take for the resonator to heal him? How long!" Charlene inquired.

"No Charlene, we have no moral obligation here, his tumor had nothing to do with us. Finding out about it here was only the discovery, not the cause," Denis suggested.

"Time in the stream of the resonator alone won't cure it," Jennifer added. "The growth is expository in nature; it will grow back as soon as he leaves. Unless we make him a member, he's dead. The question remains, does he fit in? Not whether we should cure him or not; and Carl, you know that better than any of us."

With the pros and cons put forward, the time had come for a vote. The collective would adhere to the majority consensus. Hanging in the balance was me. Was I going to live or was my oncoming destiny to be one filled with hopelessness, depression and despondency?

Waiting for Charlene's return had me in turmoil. A nervous energy coursing thru me as never before; I could only relate it to what a prisoner on death row must feel like when awaiting the decision of a governors' reprieve. Stay the execution, or fry him; that was me all right. A prisoner of my own ignorance! {Ignorance is bliss}

Chapter 25

An explanation was long overdue and quite frankly expected when General Cobbs arrived at the naval base in Pensacola, Florida. Unwilling to wait for his first hand report, he was flown by order of the President from his one room penthouse aboard the Presidio to the base, where awaiting him sat the entire Presidential committee. Understanding there was going to be a flurry of tough questions directed to him, and having no other solutions as to the cause of the events that transpired back in the triangle.

Feeling dejected he limped into the meeting room with his self-confidence depleted and under duress. Sizing up the characters which made up the committee, he found optimism in the eyes of his good friends and battled scared companions Generals Kielipper and Filston. Before Cobbs reached the circular solid oak table, his allies Kielipper and Filston stood up and gestured a welcoming handshake.

"She was a tough one wasn't she Ken!" directed General Kielipper.

"Boys you have no idea!" stated Cobbs.

""Better you than me Ken," laughed General Filston.

"We can all be thankful you weren't heading the mission," Cobbs smarted back.

The three amigos joined in a stress releasing laugh before taking their seats. Immediately upon their asses hitting the wooden surface of the chairs, the door to the conference room sprang open. All the parties lurched up to their feet as the President entered the room. 'Good morning Mr. President' could be heard from across the hall. The President calmly walked up to General Cobbs. Unsure of the President's philosophy; as it pertained to the degree of responsibility Cobbs had to atone for, the General expected a verbal thrashing to commence forthwith. In a surprising twist of compassion, the President looked Cobbs square in the face and reached his hand out in a gesture of thankfulness.

"Let me congratulate you on a job well done General. Keeping your composure under that sort of pressure must have been hard to command, well done sir well done."

The President set the mode for the meeting with his understanding of how General Cobbs had no way of controlling the situation on the Presidio. The rest of the cabinet fell in line accordingly. When the meeting concluded, a positive and definite directive was put forth by the President; it was as follows:

Until now the United States of America has never backed down to an unknown force. It is with a vast belief that to do so in this instance will not only forgo an unnecessary risk to the men and women who protect this great nation of ours but will serve as notice that not all things placed here by God are to be solved or understood. For that very reason the United States will deem this area off limits to all and every convoy. Be it by air or sea, until a time when this area and its abnormality could be fully defined and understood. We cannot take the chance of an arbitrary launch onto our own soil by our own weapons. This is not a recommendation, it is law; by the power of the President under home land security.

As the session came to a close and the parties all dispersed, the three Generals stood among themselves alone along the corridor wall. They were waiting silently in the wake, until all the traffic was gone and there were no unwanted ears probing around.

"Ok Ken what the hell happened out there, and don't give me some God dam fairy dust theory!" General kielipper demanded.

"Guys I don't know what it was or where it came from. But I've never been so fucking scared in my entire life. We lost all communications in a period of one second. Before I could call up the security clearance code, my missiles were being armed."

"Your missiles were being armed? What do you mean your missiles were being armed?" General Filston remarked hysterically.

"Yes, just what I said!" Cobbs repeated.

"That's impossible, that can't happen Ken…..could it?" Derek asked soberly.

"It's not supposed to but it did. I'll say this, gentlemen, orders or no orders I'll never enter that vector again!" General Cobbs informed them.

"Area fifty-two boys! Area fifty-two!" General Filston repeated.

"Lets hope not, but I just don't know. Keep it tight my friends; remember, we are the last defense," Cobbs said as he slowly turned to walk away.

Unable to walk three steps before General Derek Kielipper reached out and grabbed his arm saying. "Hey Ken! For real………."

Cobbs looked straight thru him and replied……… "Yes for real!"

Chapter 26

That morning brought to it a new defining aspect to Mickey's life. He had come full circle so to speak. With the beautiful and charming Ann asleep beside him, her funky bouquet from their midmorning romp lingered in the air. Spooning in bed left Mickey in a state of unfamiliar territory. He never experienced that kind of connection with a woman before. Sure he'd had all sorts of somnolent affairs, all too laborious to be counted as special. But here, with Ann, he found a contemporarily innovative love. The one attribute to his character that Mickey held true to was his affection for the purity; perhaps the very reason he never sought out a relationship with another woman. Being satisfied with the strays of the night was enough because he himself didn't feel distinguished or gallant enough to desire better, much less deserve better. That was no longer a harsh reality for Mickey, Ann saw to that.

About mid-afternoon they finally decided to join the rest of the world, leaving their sinful exploits to the memory of the bed but not before giving it another session to remember them by. They playfully enjoyed showering together as they broaden their intimacy level yet again. One could well imagine the tight fit in the shower with that Goliath taking up most of the room himself. Besides, in addition to themselves Ann took that opportunity to bring a chair into the shower with them for one final blast of exotica.

Jason amused himself in the family room playing with one of Mason's video games. Cindy sat in the dinning room reading the collective works of 'Andy Morrisette', a poet known for writing about his romantic interludes while traveling down the Mediterranean Sea. She liked the anecdotes he conveyed in his story lines. Mickey was the first to descend downstairs, close behind him trotted Ann, both boasting a smile visible from a hundred feet. Cindy caught a glimpse of Ann as she walked up to her. It didn't take Cindy long to come up with a wise crack to illustrate what Ann had just experienced.

"Having a hard time walking there girlfriend?" Cindy joked.

"Oh yah you know it!" Ann answered.

"Sooooo...... how was he?"

"Cindy!" Ann snapped as she slapped her shoulder.

"What, I'm just curious, come' on share!" she begged.

"The only thing I'm going to say is wow!"

As the two girls giggled that girly giggle, Mickey went into the family room to see Jason. Being the kind of guys they were there was no need for an explanation. Jason made a simple guy nod acknowledging Mickey's adventure and allowed him the time to enjoy his thoughts. Sitting watching Jason play the video games gave him time to bask in the moment of enjoyment and bring back to mind the after thoughts of making love. The exhaustion clearly taking its toll on him and in need of a nap, he drifted off to the sound of the video game ringing in his ears. Silence was not needed as fatigue found its way thru the obstructing noise. Jason noticed his large employee, now turned friend, had dozed off so he shut off the game and returned to the dining room to join the girls. Walking thru the hallway he could hear the faint sounds of Cindy and Ann speaking. Unable to distinguish the topic of the conversation from that distance it soon came in loud and clear when he reached the table.

"Is that all you girls talk about is sex?" he asked smiling.

"Not the only thing but one of the better things," Cindy said lifting her eyebrows at Jason inviting him to their own romp.

Ann noticed the gesture immediately and took flight, leaving her friends to assume the pleasures she had just experienced. With the only advice she could render….. "Have fun you two; don't do anything I wouldn't do."

Jason and Cindy smirked at each other as they stood up and started to walk to the stairs that led to their bedroom. Jason knew Cindy's rhythm quite well. He knew what to say and what not to say. Knowing a shot of humor was going to put her over the top, he slapped her wonderfully round ass saying "I guess its contagious lover."

Appreciating his spontaneity, she grabbed for his zipper and responded "I'll show you how contagious it really is big guy."

Ann took off in search of Mickey. Finding him asleep on the sofa, she stopped and gazed at him for a few minutes. She didn't want to wake him up but she had the craving to hold him so she slipped up beside him and crawled under his huge arms nestling close into his chest. He wiggled a little bit still slumbering allowing Ann to get comfortable. Feeling safe and secure she promptly fell asleep within his grasp, confidently huddling him.

That night the two couples planned a dinner together. It was a kind of rekindling merriment for Jason and Cindy as well as a coming of age type of gala, pertaining to the newly advanced romantically enhanced relationship between Ann and Mickey. Indulging in easy conversation about his daily routine, Mickey and Jason tossed around the idea of putting in a topical view surveillance camera. A very costly project for the common man however for Jason, it wasn't even a drop in the bucket. When it came to electrical devices and things of that nature in general, Jason was made an easy sell. It didn't matter if the object he was purchasing had any use to him or not, he was buying it. That kind of drove Cindy off the deep end once in a while, not because of the money he blew but the clutter it caused scattered all over the place. Their garage was packed to the gills with devices of all sorts that never even seen the light of day, never been taken out of the box. Cindy would complain about it in the early years but for the most part she just let him do his thing so long as it stayed in the garage.

Ann was busy preparing her first dinner for her newly acquired beau. Cindy stood steadfast at her side dedicated to helping her friend create a tantalizing treat for him. Gabbing about their sexual escapade they'd enjoyed earlier that morning and afternoon, they wanted to give the boys a special reminder of how they felt about it. Every woman knows the best way to accomplish such a task is thru the venue of food. After all they were men and not very difficult to figure out as we all have the same characteristics when it comes to our bellies. A man could forgo almost any excessive expenditure of a woman if it is presented after a great meal. That's just the way we are. I truly believe they know that fact as well. This wasn't that kind of dinner but rather the kind in which to express thanks for a remarkable day. Jason and Mickey had nothing more to do than to soak up the generosity the women were preparing for them.

The completed banquet had been served and the girls had changed into extremely sexy outfits. The men also found the need to impress the girls and to reciprocate the gesture, they too were dressed in formal suits. This particular dinner had all the makings of a gallant affair save the orchestra of a crowd. The champagne flowed freely as did the intimate indulging of dance. They mingled amongst one another finding a variety of varied topics to discuss. Speaking one on one, and at times collectively, they passed the night away entranced with each others' company. There was certainly an aura of unity shared by the four. As the night progressed, Jason and Cindy had been talking to each other about Mason. Ann had walked over to join their conversation as did Mickey.

"You never did tell me where Mason took off to Cindy," Ann commented.

"Well the truth be known Ann, we're not supposed to tell anybody about it. It's all kind of hush, hush," Cindy answered.

Taking a look at each other, Jason then decided to inform his friends of the situation concerning Mason. He gave them detailed information as he was led to believe them to be. He talked for almost an hour straight explaining each of the decisions they had to make and the agony concerning them before he finally concluded his take on the topic. Unsure how to receive this startling revelation, Ann and Mickey both gestured an indication of recognition to his openness and honesty, reassuring him of keeping the conversation clandestine.

The party ended soon after. Jason and Cindy retired to their bedroom while Mickey and Ann decided to take a walk in the backyard to get some air. They walked around the pool area hand in hand not really saying too much when all of a sudden Mickey blurted.

"Can you believe that shit?"

"It's hard to Mickey," Ann answered. "But I've known them to long not to believe them."

Ann suddenly felt a chill run down her back. She stopped dead in her tracks and stood there stiff as a board. She looked dazed and confused then helplessly dropped down to her knees.

"Ann what's wrong, are you all right?" the startled Mickey asked as he reached out to break her fall.

She said nothing for a few minutes as she just sat there on the grass thus elevating the concern level in Mickey to the point of alarm. Ann was mulling over an incident she had experienced with Steve which brought her to the realization that Jason and Cindy could very well be serious. She decided to share her discovery with Mickey.

"I'm going to tell you about something Mickey that I'm not sure you'll want to hear," she said hesitantly.

"Please go ahead Ann; I don't want anything to come between us. I'd like to be as open and honest as we can with each other. Isn't that the way it's supposed to be?" he suggested.

"Ok Mickey, about three years ago my old boyfriend Steve was working on his lawnmower, when he cut his left arm really bad. He went to hospital and got the stitches he needed and returned to his house. I was there to take care of him because the gash was so deep and so long, it took thirty-four stitches to close his wound. The very next day he was leaving for one of his trips, like he often did, and would be gone for a week or so. He would never tell me where or why he was going just that he was going. On that trip he was gone for six days. When he returned I went to see him as usual and I'll never forget what I saw as long as I lived."

"What, what did you see?" he asked curiously.

"Mickey, aside from a little scar running the entire length of his arm, there was no cut. Absolutely no cut! It was as if it was an old battle wound from years past."

"Really Ann, are you serious?" Mickey gasped.

"Yes I am Mickey, don't you see, it's the same thing with Mason and his disease. When I asked him about the cut, he said it was a Chinese remedy. When I pressed him to divulge more about it, he got defensive and told me to shut it. So I did, but never forgot it. I'm telling you he knew something about the Shield or what ever it's called!"

"Wow, I think you should let Jason and Cindy know what you know Ann, I mean it's their kid over there!" Mickey proposed.

"I will Mickey, first thing in the morning, I defiantly will," she deduced.

She picked herself up with Mickey's help, and they once again started to walk towards the entrance of the house. Wanting to change the subject to a more immediate concern she asked Mickey smiling,

"You're place or mine?"

They shared a little chuckle and Mickey replied.

"How about mine this time?"

"Sure why not, I could use a change of scenery," she laughed.

Chapter 27

Instantly, I could tell the news wasn't favorable as soon as Charlene walked in. The stealthy meeting concerning my fate had obviously gone in the wrong direction, to place such a somber, subdued look in her face. Without a word being spoken, I suddenly became aware of the imminent position I was facing. Without the Shield's healing capacity to avert and dispose of the tumor waiting to erupt in my head, the prospect of my recovery was dismal at best. In actuality, I had no chance of survival. I tried to remain calm as not to upset Charlene any more than she already was. I stood up from my bed and approached her with my arms wide opened, extending an 'I know you did your best' gesture however that didn't unburden her. She dragged herself to my bed and sat down placing her hands to cover up her face. She was clearly distraught and a bit more than agitated over the meeting.

Unexpectedly, she stood up and crossed her arms in front of her. Anger filtered with resentment had taken the place of sadness.

"Well Mike, there's only one other solution to this dilemma," she stated.

"And that would be what?" I asked.

"They're leaving me with no other choice but to give you your own schematic so you can build a resonator of your own," she explained.

"My own resonator, how can I build a resonator Charlene? I mean how could I?" I questioned.

"I'll get you everything you'll need to put together one of your own. All you'll have to do is get the material and assemble it. Mike it's the only way you'll live," she said

"I know that but do you think they will allow you to give me that."

"We're not going to tell them Mike. This is going to stay between you and me. There's just one thing you must promise; you can never divulge the resonator to anyone, not one single solitary soul can learn of it Mike. If they did, the result would be catastrophic!"

That moment I realized the devotion and commitment Charlene had for me. She really did love me and would do anything to show it. Hardly does a man find such true conviction in a partner in life. I knew it was not a possibility for her to join me but that didn't dissuade her from doing what was best for me. By all accounts she would remain the love of my life even if she wasn't going to share in the day to day aspects of it; her devotion and trust would remain a part of me for all time; I trust her memory of me would be the same.

We spent the remaining time together, holding each other and giving support to one another as the time for my departure closed near. Having fallen asleep curled up in each other's arms; we were awoken by the shake and rattle of what I could only perceive as the rising of the Shield to the surface. Charlene confirmed my presumption while she suggested I prepare to confront Carl. She had explained to me previously that the others would be giving me a warning not to converse or even contemplate the idea of discussing the Shield to anybody from the outside world. As predicted, that very warning was issued. Standing before me were Carl, Jennifer, the huge guy Leo and Charlene. It was a sobering moment to be sure, and I asked if I'd see any of them again, 'not likely' was the response I got from Jennifer. I walked slowly as possible to the giant stainless steel door that led to the surface and paused to ingest the last lingering scent of Charlene's perfume. Then from out of the shadows Mason came running up towards me shouting 'Uncle Mike, Uncle Mike." My heart instantly soared with the reminiscing words of Mason saying 'Uncle Mike'. Stopping short of running me down Mason wrapped his arms around me and said.

"Take care Uncle Mike and don't forget, I'm where I want to be, doing the best thing I can for myself."

Handing me a folded piece of paper, he asked me to give to his mom and dad; he turned and walked away, never even looking back. Charlene waved her hand across the beam that activated the opening of the door and we walked out of the Shield together. Feeling the upward thrush of surfacing, I quickly turned to Charlene and kissed her. A sudden jerk and the door to the outside opened. The stench in the air instantly burned thru my nostrils causing me to cough.

"This is as far as I can go Mike," she said as she began to sob.

"I know my love. I just wish I could take you with me," I answered.

"Please remember me and never forget that I love you," she whispered in my ear.

"Never Charlene, never," I said.

"Take this Mike, and be well, remember also your promise," she spoke as she handed me a small disk.

"I will my love," I insisted.

She stepped back into the door and as I helplessly watched it close, I felt the sorrow impact my soul forthwith. I stumbled to the jumbo jet waiting for me to board and took one last look around at the deserted tarmac. With a faint of heart I entered and took a seat overlooking the airstrip. As we took off I was overcome with emotion and started to cry for I knew this was the last time I would ever see my beloved Mason or cherished Charlene again.

When the plane landed, I was escorted off by the pilot. He walked with me down the corridor of the on/off ramp remaining silent. When we arrived at the terminal gate, as I walked thru, he turned and proceeded directly back. Once again I found myself amid thousands of strangers at the International Airport in St Paul Minnesota. The same people walking by, busy with their every day travels. Yes, the same people, doing the same thing, wearing the same clothes, yakking about the same troubles, everything was exactly the same………….. Except me!

The car ride back to Greenbush was long and drawn out. It did give me some time to adjust so to speak to the environment. I thought it funny in a way. Back in the Shield, I couldn't remember ever looking upwards, but here there was the sky, clouds drifting by, the tall pine trees bending as the wind took hold of their outreached branches, and the sway of the scrub weeds which lined the highway dancing in the breeze………..I was home.

A desperate feeling of need scuttled thru me as I became more and more aware of the confrontation I had to face. Jason and Cindy were the only friends I had left. I had let them down in such an immense way; I couldn't envision any circumstance that would render them anything other than hostile. Cindy for certain will want me executed or hung while Jason will most likely kick my ass back to the Stone Age. Mostly though, I was disappointed in myself. I decided to first go to my own house, change and prepare for what I had to do. I thought it better to just show up rather than call ahead so I didn't have to explain anything over the phone.

Oh my God, oh my God, I repeated to myself, while standing outside Jason's front door.

"Yes can I help you?" the big man said.

"Oh, I'm here to see Jason or Cindy," I answered. "Say is your name Mickey?" I asked recognizing him immediately.

"Yes it is, oh you're Mike, please come in, come in," he repeated.

"Is Jason about?" I asked.

"Sure, he's in the backyard swimming I believe," Mickey said.

I was puzzled to be certain that Mickey had answered the door. What the hell was he doing here and more importantly, why? I remembered we'd used his services for going out but never at our homes. He led me outside just in time to view Jason make a double summersault off the diving board. When he came up from the water I instinctively blurted "You never could get that dive right jay man!"

"Mike! What the hell are you doing back? When did you get back? Hey, where's Mason?"

I didn't answer him right away. Passing him a towel I suggested that we go inside to talk. I also asked if Cindy was home but before Jason could utter a word she came running out of the pool house yelling my name.

"Well, well, well, if it isn't our guardian angel," she said as she approached me.

"It's so good to see you both," I said "and I hope your attitude stays the same when I tell you what I have to tell you!"

"Tell us what Mike, where's Mason?" Jason asked firmly this time.

"Let's go inside guys, what I'm going to say will be quite a shock."

"No Mike! Here, now, where is my son!" Cindy demanded.

"Ok Cindy, please just calm down. Mason is at the Shield. He's safe and is getting better everyday," I explained.

Reaching into my pocket I pulled out the folded letter Mason had given me to give to his parents.

"He wanted me to give you this," I said as I handed the letter to Cindy.

Holding the letter close to her heart like it was Mason himself, she slowly rubbed the epistle in a circling motion across her chest. Unable to open it, she handed the only connection to her son over to Jason who himself was visibly shaken up. As he opened the letter, his eyes swelled up and tears began flowing down his flushed cheeks when he read............

"My dearest Mom and Dad:

I hope I find you well and in good spirits. I can imagine the pain and stress you must be under not having me there to protect. I must tell you in light of the marvelous things I've encountered here at the Shield; nothing could take the place in my heart as the both of you.

You held me tight to yourselves when I woke up scared in the middle of the night and never left my side when I was sick. You've placed my wants and my needs ahead of your own and for that I will be eternally grateful. Having grown up with you, I learned a great deal of what it means to be happy. The good times were certainly first-class while the bad times paled in comparison.

If I could only describe this place so you could better understand the truly amazingly, incredible world that exists here, I'm sure you'd approve of my desire to stay. Mom, Dad, please understand that I'd never want to hurt you for any reason, but I could by no account go back to believing the lies accepted by the world as fact when knowing all along it was nothing but nonsense.

In some way my understanding of how the natural order of things are supposed to progress have been enhanced to an unbelievable level to which extent I haven't even pinnacled as of yet. Rest assured I will advance in the knowledge and understanding of what I was born to realize.

Now, please don't blame Uncle Mike for any of this. He had no preconceived knowledge of the circumstances that would follow bringing me here. He just wanted to help and by all accounts he did that very thing. Mom, I'll never be sick again. Dad, in time I will expand the Shield to encompass the understanding of harmony for all mankind. Is that not a justified and noble cause worth pursuing? To me it has to be, for it is my destiny.

I love you both very much and wish that your life be filled to capacity with the joy and bliss knowing I've attained the unattainable.

Your son
With love and hope,
"Mason"

Attempting not to look at Cindy, I couldn't help but hear her gut wrenching wailing as Jason read the letter. Wanting to comfort her, I reached to embrace her to further extenuate my actions. However, she brashly swept away my approach and willfully slapped the right side of my face.

"You fucking bastard!" she yelled. "How could you? You son of a bitch! You took him away, you took him away!" she continued screaming.

I immediately turned to Jason for some understanding but was met with a stern and abrasive stare. Having no other retreat available, I could only hold my ground and accept that which was coming.

"You'd better leave Mike, right now!" Jason commanded.

"Jason, I didn't want any of this to happen you know that. Come on, you have to know that!" I begged.

"Just leave Mike! Get out of my sight," he directed.

Leaving as ordered, a somber, crushing ambiance followed me out the door. Wrapped in anguish and incapable of holding my emotions intact, I broke down even before reaching the consolatory safety of my car. My knees buckled as my eyes strained to find my way back to where I had parked. Piercing thru the haze of stinging water impairing my vision, I finally acquired a lock to its position. Stumbling around my pockets in a frantic search for my keys, I clutched them and proceeded to unlock the door. In a dire state of emotional deprivation, with the weight of responsibility having caused my dearest and longest lasting friend such horrifically, dreadful sorrow, the thought of driving off a cliff ending this miserable existence actually came to mind. I felt broken, desolate, bereft of everything I'd held of value.

Not knowing or too inept to remember how I returned home, I soon found myself sitting in my driveway, apparently having plowed my Hummer directly thru the black spiraled steel gate guarding my home. Surrounded by the smoke and debris from the concrete being shattered and sent flying in all directions, it didn't take long for a crowd to assemble. Ashamed and embarrassed I sprinted to my house for the security and serenity that would not only shelter me but seclude me from the curiosity of the unwanted on lookers. Once inside I locked the door and stumbled to the kitchen were I fell to the floor and lay doubled over wincing in pain. I didn't realize it at the time but I had broken my arm in two places in the accident. It wasn't until I went to hospital that I found out the degree of my injury. Of course as with any car accident the doctors wanted to be very thorough and precise as to any injury. They ran all kinds of x-rays, M.R.I.'s and a C.A.T. scan. When they finally finished Doctor Marcien Courshene came in to deliver his diagnosis.

"Well Mr. James, you have broken your left arm in two places. That will heal as we have set the arm and you'll be placed in a cast for approximately eight weeks," he said.

"Thanks doc, does that mean I can go home when it's done?" I asked

"Not really Mr. James. The C.A.T. scan showed some very troubling images. I'd like to run a few more tests to be completely certain of what we think we saw, is actually what is showing up," he informed me.

"Are you referring to the tumor Doctor Courshene?" I inquired.

"What, you know about it Mr. James?" he answered.

"Yes I do, don't waste your time doc, there's nothing you can do for me. Nothing anyone could do for me," I commented.

Returning home it came to me, if there was going to be any hope in a recovery from this tumor I was going to have to build the resonator. A job not well suited for a man with only one working arm. I decided to hire a few, shall we say less than prominent workers to assemble different parts of the resonator. Over the next couple of weeks I made arrangements for all the components needed to assemble it. The scheduling alone took more than its fair share of my time but was necessary to ensure complete and absolute anonymity. At no time were the different workers that were needed allowed to be working at the same interval. My entire basement was used for the location of the resonator. That had allowed me to separate the working areas over the entire seven thousand square feet encompassing the lowest level of my home. Reading the schematic came relatively easy; the design of the apparatus was simple for such a powerful unit. The difficulty lay in the arrangement of the magnets. Each one of the six thousand, four hundred and forty- four 2 ½ x 2 1/2 x 1 inch magnets had to be calibrated to within one-one thousandths of an inch to its counter part to create the perpetual motion. If one of the magnets was off by as much as a hair, the jig was up. That meant recalibrating the entire system again right from scratch.

The lanky, tedious task had almost come to fruition when a startling thought came to mind. If this machine did work, how in God's name could I ever explain my sudden rejuvenation? The Shield had no worries of hiding its incredible affects, however; I wasn't going to be sheltered from the curiosities of the media or the bombardment of the constant borage of questions that would surely follow. A heightened degree of security was definitely called for and certainly necessary if the surreptitious nature of the resonator was to remain just that, covert.

Chapter 28

To this point, neither Jason nor Cindy found the time or the necessity in having any contact with me. I was left alone to deal with my illness like an abandoned tribe, tagged as a leper colony. For that insipid reason, it came as a downright surprise when Jason showed up at my door some six weeks later!

Surprised can't even come close to how I felt. Here I was facing the dilemma of a life time; all the while my best friend, with whom I should be extracting courage from, is treating me like a second class citizen. If ever I was elated to see someone, it was Jason that morning!

Excitedly opening the door before he had a chance to knock, I boyishly jumped into his arms, thrilled at seeing my playmate once again.

"Jason, I can't tell you how good it is to see you, please come in!" I said gleefully.

"Thanks Mike, how've you been?" he asked.

"Well buddy, the truth is I'm one sick puppy," I stated.

"Sick? What do you have, a cold or something?" he inquired.

"I wish Jay, no, I found out I have a tumor the size of a grapefruit in my head," I informed him.

"Are you kidding? That's not funny Mike, not funny at all!" he barked.

"I'm serious Jason," I told him as we walked over to the sofa.

"When did this happen?" he asked.

I didn't want to bring up the avenue where I found out about the tumor but I was left with no other choice. This could have been a huge mistake, given the fact I hadn't seen him since the conflict at his house however I answered his question.

"One of the last days I was at the Shield, Charlene had informed me of it. She told me if not taken care of, I wouldn't see another birthday." I said.

"Well what are the doctors saying, there must be something they could do!" he responded.

"No, not a thing Jason, they can't do a thing for me."

Jason took on a look of pure disbelief. He pressingly felt horrible for not coming over sooner. I could tell by his slouch, the amount of regret he was enduring for that decision was weighing heavily on him. I didn't want him to feel any remorse for that so I informed him that I had a plan in the works to combat my illness.

"So what are you going to do Mike?"

I knew and remembered I had given my word to Charlene, not to divulge any information about having a resonator. However, this was Jason, not only did he know about it at the Shield, he also lost his son to it and I deemed it ok to tell him of our secret. He didn't believe me at first so I brought him to the basement and showed him the results of six weeks work. The resonator took all but a few inches of the total height of the room. It stood eleven feet tall and sixteen feet wide. The combined weight of the unit, along with the absorption chamber came in at just under forty-four thousand pounds. I explained how I had to reinforce the floor to compensate for the deflection of vibration that would have normally shaken the house to a pile of rubble. Jason being quite a moderately intellectual himself found the concept and design easy to understand. I explained how the contraption worked and he clued in right away.

"All I have to do is stay within the field for ten hours a day for the pulse of the resonator to shrink the tumor. Charlene had told me it might take as long as six months to completely dissipate it. Seeing as though I'm not using the resonator for energy, all the power is being concentrated on an extraction pulse, multiplying the effectiveness ten fold. I haven't as yet turned it on; I was waiting for the right time. So what do you think Jason?" I probed.

"Well Mike, the old saying is 'there's no time like the present,'" he said smirking.

I took a deep breath, exhaled, looked Jason in the eyes and threw the switch.

A low toned hum as if the resonator was jammed, excreted from within the unit. Without warning it jumped into high gear as the shock absorbers surrounding it started to vibrate. Jason and I looked at each other, uncertain what to think. The glow filling the chamber had the same features as the Shield itself. By all accounts, according to Charlene, all that was necessary to commence the regeneration process was to enter the absorption chamber. I read the override terminal to indicate whether or not it was safe to proceed. Everything seemed fine, all systems checked out ok. I asked Jason to keep his eye on the terminal, just in case something happens in which I couldn't evacuate the pod quick enough if trouble arose. So throwing caution in the wind, I entered.

The effects took hold instantly. I felt the rays penetrate my skin filling my body with a sensation even stronger than experienced at the Shield. Perhaps the pure concentration of energy was uniquely formatting to a singular purpose. Either way, the magnetic field pulse was doing its job, of that I was certain. I stepped out of the absorption chamber feeling like a new man. Jason asked how I was, concerned about the whole thing. I tried to reassure him everything was working just as it was supposed to.

"Would you like to try it out Jay?" I asked him.

"No Mike, that's fine," he answered hesitantly.

"Really Jason it's ok to use. It kind of feels like getting tickled all over your body at the same time; but without the laughing," I said.

"Mike something has to be wrong, just look at the sweat pouring off of you. I think you better forget this thing!" he exclaimed.

"Ha, ha, ha no Buddy that is exactly what's supposed to happen. All this sweat isn't just sweat. It's the impurities in my blood filtering out thru the pores of my body is all, that's how it works," I explained.

"What's that smell Mike? It reminds me of….."

"Yah I know, smells like jasmine right? That's why I know it's working as well, that's the smell of the Shield."

Jason smiled acknowledging and confirming his belief that the resonator had been assembled correctly. He was tentative moreover a tad bit speculative but he at last decided to give it a whirl. Cautiously creeping up, like a baby summoning the courage to take its first step, he dawdled his way to the entrance of the absorbing chamber, gradually opening the door and sluggishly sauntered on in. Taking a seat in the extra large leather lounger, then promptly putting his feet up, his demeanor vastly changed. The timidly apprehensive Jason had left. In his place sat a confident, robust Jason.

"Wow, Mike this is fantastic!" he exclaimed.

"Yes it sure is something," I answered.

According to the schematic, it was possible to allow the flow of resonator to encapsulate the entire house. That would lessen the amount of time I would need to spend in the chamber. The danger lay in prospect of someone else finding out about it. That would mean no persons what so ever could visit my residence again. Not that I had many people over anyway, being a recluse in that matter was beneficial. So again, I let caution flare and opened the door to allow the magnetic pulse to circulate thought-out my home. Jason, meanwhile basking in the stream so to speak, made it perfectly clear he wanted one.

"Mike you have to let me build one of these at my place," He demanded.

"I can't Jason, I just can't. I gave my word not to divulge any of this."

"I understand that but that doesn't include me does it? I mean hell; we already know about it, we already sent our son there, what's the difference?" he argued.

A suitable riposte was not available to me. I couldn't come up with a reason other than giving my word to Charlene. Talk about a conflict, here I was with my best friend arguing a point that I myself didn't believe in. We had the means of ending the entire world's dependency on fossil fuels, on any type of energy really. The resonator could be built on a city wide basis, all across the world, providing a clean and inexhaustible source of power, not to mention the heath benefits that would avail it self to the masses. The more and more I thought about it, the more I was convinced I was right. Perhaps the reason the Shield didn't want this secret out was straight forward. They enjoyed the prestige of having a dominate society, sickness free, with the power to orchestrate the dominion over mankind.

"No Jason! I'm not going to allow you to have one of these!" I decided.

"What do you mean Mike? How could you not want us to benefit from this? I don't understand your thinking!" he yelled.

"Jason you are right! This is something the whole world should have access to. And I'm going to make sure they do. You know, I've never understood why I was fortunate enough to have had the tremendous affluence I've acquired, I think now I do. Maybe it was destiny maybe it was kismet, either way I know what I must do."

"Way to go Mike, that's the ticket. The world should have this available to them!" he agreed.

HIND SIGHT IS 20/20……………………..

Chapter 29

In light of which, I was the rich and powerful Mike Robert James, inventor of the may-moo security device, billionaire extraordinaire; the media was all abuzz with the news of a new discovery on tap. Jason and I agreed to keep it to ourselves where the resonator originated from. Cindy, Ann, and Mickey were the only other people with some knowledge of the Shield and they were onboard as well. We decided not to try to make money but to release it to the public in an open form so as not to allow any corporation to corrupt this technology. This was to be available to all people, on all continents, for everyone to benefit.

It took some time to develop and a few problems arose with the construction of a resonator ten times the size of my own however, in the months that followed, we methodically and meticulously worked it out. The time to disclose the mystery was upon us.

There was a representative from each and every network standing center stage for our presentation. We billed the event as the most remarkable and beneficial discovery of all time. Thousands had gathered to hear and view the incredulous finding. Walking up to the podium, my nervousness had gripped its hold on me. Taking a sip of water to clear my throat and to calm myself, I began…….

"Ladies and gentlemen, I want to thank you for taking the time to be here with us, as we prepare to enter an exciting and unforgettable era for the human race. Firstly allow me to say, it is with great pleasure I introduce the co-founder of this experiment, my friend and long time business partner Jason Tanndy.

For many years now the economy and social order has been buckling at the knees over two very diverse and yet connected issues. That of energy and health care. What we have to present to the world could only be described as a miracle. Let us take energy and we shall get to the medical circumstance next.

The apparatus standing behind me is called a reverse magnetic polarity resonator. Its design is very complicated and difficult to explain, so I won't even try to. What I will explain is the effect to our everyday lives this will have. Upon releasing the blueprints to the resonator, which is our intent, the governments of the globe will have no choice but to provide this system to all its citizens respectfully. Behind me is a power generator if you will. It will produce enough energy to sustain an entire city the size of Greenbush. For bigger cities the design need only to be enlarged accordingly. There are no emissions, none what's so ever, nor is there a need for panic over nuclear fallout. The only emitted particle of this mechanism is that of benefit. Oddly enough, that brings us to the next topic; that of health care.

For some of us suffering from one kind of sickness or debilitating disease, this is a medical miracle. We have discovered a way to harness the energy that is produced within the magnetic field which is so intense, so concentrated, that the properties of the field can and will influence the regular stream of flow thru a person's body. Once exposed to the pulse, the body automatically starts the rejuvenation process. What does this mean? To put it frankly, any, and to this point, all impurities that live within a blood cell are excreted thru the pores of the body, thus leaving only healthy, pure, and clean cells. No more sickness. No more disease, not so much as a pimple from this time on. Now of course the F.D.A. will certainly want to ensure the resonator is safe and in no way could possibly harm anybody. This is a natural process that will have to be studied. I'm here to assure you, that it is completely safe and even if the governments don't want you to enjoy and reap the rewards of this mind boggling technology, it will be made available by way of internet at the conclusion of this conference. We feel it is necessary to avoid the congestion of those who'd take this system and pervert it to a money making scheme, over those who couldn't otherwise afford to build it. Making it available to all is the only way to ensure everyone is given the same opportunity to benefit. Now, as for the precaution of ensuring this isn't perverted in anyway, we've left out one of the main focal points to the construction of the resonator. Why? It's simple.

Before a constructed resonator could be placed as operational, our own team of engineers will make the trip at our expense to ensure its safety. We have sixty qualified people ready to take on this enormous task. Rest assured we will press the governments to qualify as many others as is necessary to complete this globally. We only ask for your patience in this matter as we deal with the volume of inquiries. At this point I'd invite you all to feel free to look at and explore the resonator. Thank you."

With all the phone calls and media beating down our doors, we found it too overwhelming to remain at our respective homes. We took off in our company jet to outwait the endless stream of questions directed to us from every government on the planet. We left Terry Burns, our oldest and most experienced lawyer to deal with the fallout. The news as you could imagine flowed rapidly throughout the world. Overnight it seemed millions of resonators had been attempted to be built. It came as no surprise to us the amount of urgency some would have to build these units; the rich certainly had the advantage at first. As supplies grew shorter and shorter, as was the aim here in controlling the amounts of units able to be constructed, the population grew more and more restless.

Thinking this was going to be a momentary upraising of dissonance, we stayed the course we set out to maintain. We brought as many resonators on line as possible. The governments, to no avail, did everything in their power to discourage the building of these units as it was causing mass amounts of people to forgo their normal daily routine of work and services. The impact to everyday life was mayhem to its max. The amount of unemployment produced within the energy industry was phenomenally underestimated. By the time we tried to avert any other systems from coming on line, it was too late. I guess we never took into account all the different industries that would be affected by the release of this technology.

The separation in classes grew dramatically over the period of six months. Before the year was over, a staggering estimation of fifty-five percent of all people globally, were either out of work or uninterested in finding work. A calamity of unknown proportions was about to show its ugly face, as we were helpless to stop it. There remained only two classes of society at this point. The truly rich! And the truly needy! This situation was not only indicative of the United States, but eclipsed every nation in the same fashion. What Jason and I regarded as a world saving power was ending up just like Charlene had warned. A complete and total catastrophe!

It wasn't as if every person on earth wanted our heads on a platter, no far from it. The rich indulged in a life of pleasures never experienced before. It was one thing to have money, but to have money, health and the opportunity to have it all for the rest of eternity was nothing short of heaven. It's funny how many friends one can count when giving those same friends and utopia of that sort.

The horror surrounding the disadvantaged was nothing short of terror. It was twenty years following our presentation before the complete desolation of society was realized. The men and women who controlled ninety-nine percent of the assets, that being made up of less than a half of a percent of the population, dominated the other ninety-nine and a half percent of the world. Mankind has always been a selfish and power-hungry being, however now the power-hungry were not satisfied with mere power; they needed more to entertain themselves. The resonator saw fit to enhance their desire. If one had a greedy tendency before the resonator experience, it turned to insatiable gluttony. If an individual with a passion for misconduct set foot in the resonator, his passion for misdemeanor activity turned to corrupt delinquency. The same could be said for those who enjoyed inflicting a little pain or abuse on to others, they turned into masochistic, homicidal maniacs.

With no sight of relief from the turmoil in sight, the actions set in play by Jason and I were exceedingly hard to deal with. Millions of innocent people, the majority of them kids, had suffered the indignation of a growing member of the new found extraordinarily sadistic inhabitants. Within fifty years, the fabric that once held together our fragile communities had completely broken down. There were no longer such things as elections of office, no more public protection, or even a bill of rights for that matter. The planet was basically left to be run at the discretions of a few wealthy, powerful and morally inept men and women. In former pre-resonator years, the natural diminishing of man's virility kept him closer to the bonds of marriage and family. With the virtual endless rejuvenation capability spawned by the resonators, it was all these youth seeking barons needed to find a new and reinvigorating affair that was scarcely waiting around the next corner. To an otherwise old geezer to whom a young, sexy, vigorous woman would be totally unattainable, today the possibilities were endless. They discarded the sufferings of others as that of insignificant. They themselves took particular interest in watching two innocent children fight to the death for a mere morsel of food. The corruption that enabled them to get away with these types of torture, were the same ones that looked up to them for handouts. Policing took on a new form. They were no longer the strong, brave defenders of the misfortunate or helpless. Now, this was a company of warriors, whose job it was to defend the gluttony of these outrageous, contemptible people who only took pride in the sufferings they could inflict on others. A sicker society the world has never seen.

Chapter 30

The Shield was right!

In reflection, peering out at the endless streets of mile high buildings, filled to their capacity of ageless and corrupted people, I try to recall a time of simple pleasures - A time when youth was sought after with the greatest of vigilance. Old age was feared and almost looked down upon. Most people would do anything to prevent the effects of age. Sickness and disease, which once ran rampant throughout the world, is now a faded memory. A tragedy in itself, as it was necessary. I know that now. Whatever pain or uncertainty was placed on an individual when diagnosed with a fatal or crippling disease was certainly a far better justice than we presently face. The lines between life and death, sickness and health are but a distant memory, for those of us who can remember. The last hundred and fifty years or so have past thru the river of time like a thief without remorse or conviction. The reality is that when time has no bounty on life, the impossible grants possibilities, as the unjust exploit the just. Life certainly was never meant to yield such an extravagant price. Yet the unknown had a basis worthy of that price. With all the discord and strife in the word, it was the hurts and pains that made us who we were. What's left here now is a mere shadow of life…

Still remaining one of the richest men in the state, I was able to distribute as much charity to the disadvantaged as possible. Unwilling to bend to the demands of the other wealthy individuals who suggested I let the natural order of things take over, it was made clear to me; they thought I was wasting my time and resources on an element of society not worthy of existence. Other than to appease their lust for cruelty and entertainment, the vast majority of the rich wouldn't give the time of day to help anyone. Even sicker yet, they disapproved of any generosity shown by that of their comrades. If one of the elite was seen even speaking to one of the putrid, rancid members of the lower class, they'd find themselves ostracized, and not soon after demoted to that same measure.

No longer living alone in a posh extravagant dwelling, the need for compassion soon turned my castle into a soup kitchen. I didn't have the sports cars and Rembrandts hanging from my walls. Instead, the bulk of my assets went to funding the overpopulated masses of hungry individuals that poured onto my property on a daily basis. Willing to work for the food they received by planting and watering the fifty acres of land I purchased, we made due with supplies we were able to grow. This was one of only a small handful of sanctuaries available in our state. Feeling utterly responsible for having caused this dilemma, I felt it necessary to do whatever I could to alleviate and ease the burden of suffering I had instigated.

On March 29th 2168 at precisely 8:35 am, the door bell rang and as customary I walked over to open it, expecting to find a few hungry people looking for sustenance. To my complete surprise and in total amazement, there stood Charlene and Carl.

"What are you doing here?" I asked shockingly.

"Mike, may we come in please?" Carl asked.

"Yes, please come in, make yourself at home," I pleaded.

We walked to the sitting room where we were surrounded by a dozen field workers having their breakfast. The look in Charlene's face said it all. She was insulted and angry but mostly feeling betrayed. She didn't have to say it, I already knew. I offered them something to eat or drink but they refused. They suggested I clear the room as they had something imperative to discuss with me. I did, and as the last person left the room Carl started:

"You stupid son of a bitch! How could you be so God dam dumb? We warned you of this situation before you left and you said; you gave your word not to divulge any of this. Well you stupid fuck look at you now!" he shouted.

I sat there absorbing all the abuse Carl had to throw at me. I knew dam well he was right and it was completely deserved.

"Is there anything you can do to help the situation Carl?" I pleaded.

"No! Of course not, what do you think, we have some kind of magic ball that will make all this simply disappear?" he exclaimed.

"I was hoping you might have some kind of suggestion to help is what I meant."

Charlene then said something to me that knocked me off my feet.

"Do you have any idea of the suffering you have caused Mike?" she asked.

"Yes I do Charlene, and I can't tell you how sorry I am for causing it, but what can I do but to try and change things for the better at this point."

"No Mike you don't have a clue as to what you've done!" Charlene cried.

"Charlene, I know you're hurt and disappointed in my judgment. I thought I was doing a good thing, how could I have known things would ever turn out this way?"

"We told you it would Mike. There was no other way this could possibly go. You don't think we would have liked to give help to those that need it? The fact is, that would be just as irresponsible as your decision!" she pointed out.

Carl broke in, "Mike have you any idea where all this is going to lead?"

"To be honest Carl, I don't. Not a single clue! I was hoping that if enough people protest and start standing up for what is right, things might improve."

"Mike, you have single handedly destroyed the consistency that was the moral fiber which held together the worlds only chance at attaining harmony. The fact of being mortal was the only aspect of life this putrid place could believe in. You not only took away the rights of those who strive to do well, you made this a place of constant pain and suffering. I'm ashamed I put so much faith in you Mike.......it would have been better for everyone if the tumor had exploded and left you for dead. One life is not worth the five billion you have caused and continue to cause such dire and desperate pain on a daily basis. If you really want to atone for your unconscionable actions, this is the only way. You can't see it Mike, but the billions not millions but billions of people are left starving and fighting for the simplest degree of comfort and it's all your doing."

"Do the right thing Mike, do the right thing!" she ended, while Carl handed me a disk.

When Charlene finished speaking, the impact of the situation pointed to a clear and definite path to which should to be taken. I'd noticed the disk Carl had in his hand when they came in but I wanted to wait and see if it was a solution to the problem or the means in which to end it all, the latter ended up being the truth. They both got up and walked to the door. Carl walked right out, not saying another word. Charlene turned to me one more time. Her eyes were filled with tears running down her still beautiful soft cheeks.

"End the suffering Mike, for God's sake, end the suffering!" she begged as she walked out of my life for good.

Trying to remain calm, having been told I was better off dead from the woman I had loved for over one hundred and fifty years had its own pain attached to it. The realization that she was correct in her assessment however left a bitter taste in my mouth. If indeed there was a God, then eternal damnation was certainly going to be my reward. The impact of suffering I placed on the world thru my own volition had me wishing I was never even born. My father, who'd passed on many years ago, not wanting to partake in the experience of the resonator, told me on his death bed. "Son, the more you try to discover a new and exciting possibility for life and not live the life given you, the more unfulfilling you will find it to be." He was a wise man and I should have taken his advice.

I spent the rest of that day watching the outcasts' labor in the fields in the hot afternoon sun. I looked each and every one of them up and down trying to decipher whether or not life had a fulfilling aspect to them or was it just plain miserable survival. Not one shared in a smile or laugh, the only expression on their faces was that of pain, hardship and want. If life was this bad for these people, who had food and clean water and a bed to rest in at night, I could well imagine what some or most of the other inhabitants must be enduring. Yes there was only one solution to this…..only one!

Chapter 31

That night sitting by myself in my favorite comfortable arm chair, with the thought of crawling thru another mundane day, only a few hours away, I came to the only logical conclusion left. I had no idea of how many resonators were out there circulated throughout the globe but that didn't make much of a difference at this point. According to their message on the disk, the motion of reversing the magnetic field in my own resonator would send a vibrating pulse so massively strong, it would destroy everything in its path. When reaching another resonator, it would automatically reverse the field in those as well, the result being a global reaction from one resonator to the next causing complete and unstoppable destruction. The end of mankind along with it all the suffering would be over in a matter of hours. With nowhere to run and nowhere to hide, the inevitable would approach with discriminatory force, vanquishing the rich as well as the poor; relentlessly evicting man off the face of the planet. Taking one last sip of cognac.......

SYSTEM ACTIVATED.........

10, 9, 8, 7, 6, 5, 4, 3, 2, 1 ....

Chapter 32

Streaking across the compound past the finely groomed fruit trees, Charlene hurriedly made her way to Carl's lavishly adorned hut. The only one of its kind in the entire Shield, seeing as he was known to be the leader and foremost authority left. She broke in with complete confidence and reported to him that Mike had indeed initiated the destruction sequence. Feeling proud or so it seemed he pushed out his chest as if to demonstrate his masculine victory.

"How did you know he would do it Carl?" she asked inquisitively.

"My love, a man will only do that which he is subject to do according to his opus. You know as well as I that was the very reason we brought him here to begin with. His constitution was made up of a brilliant mind suckled by an indispose capability for handling responsibility. It was the same with Steve Markinson remember? He had the same flair when it came to the unknown possibilities of accepting life here, but like you know we had to get rid of him because he didn't fit in. He wouldn't have had the guts to rid the world of life. Now Mike was a different story. When faced with the reality of a no win situation, he took the only route available, that of getting out," he explained.

"I still don't understand how you knew Carl, you're more brilliant than I ever conceived," she flattered.

Walking towards him, reaching out with her arms wide open offering a congratulatory embrace, Carl never perceived any misdoing. He simply and arrogantly reciprocated the gesture. While entangled in a warm and sultrily provocative clinch, Charlene pulled a nickel plated berretta from her side. While distracting Carl with a series of moans and groans as to indicate her arousal, the last thing to enter his head besides the bullet was the thought of what a stud he was. As he lay collapsed, Charlene exited his hut and immediately made her way to Mason's home.

Entering his hut with an entourage consisting of his father Jason, his mother Cindy and their closest friends Mickey and Ann, she said those endearing words that lingered on thru Mason's mind... "My love, we did it"............

To be continued.....{The Last Shield; The New Beginning} ....

About the Author

Mark has lived a hard and rather difficult life. Growing up on the wrong side of the tracks, where the struggle to simply 'just get by' took more than mere luck. His brand of reasoning was often mistaken as harsh or even callous at times, however, he always stood true for what he perceived as right and justly. A father of four that unfortunately had no time to enjoy the everyday interacting with his wife and kids, as he drove a truck all over God's green earth to provide his family with their daily needs, and his patrons with their daily goods. With his oldest son now eighteen, having been diagnosed with Juvenile Diabetes at the age of thirteen, gave Mark an understanding for the need to help out. That is why Mark has decided to donate 10% of his royalties from his books to the Juvenile Diabetes Society. Although he may look like a grizzly bear, a teddy bear would be more accurate.

Printed in the United States
137816LV00002B/2/A